MOUNTAIN DANGER

WILD MOUNTAIN MEN - BOOK 4

VANESSA VALE

Mountain Danger

Copyright © 2020 by Vanessa Vale

This is a work of fiction. Names, characters, places and incidents are the products of the author's imagination and used fictitiously. Any resemblance to actual persons, living or dead, businesses, companies, events or locales is entirely coincidental.

Cover design: Bridger Media

Cover graphic: Deposit Photos: EpicStockMedia

1

 VE

"YOU ARE *NOT* WEARING a Cutthroat Police shirt to my party," Poppy told me, one eyebrow raised and a finger waggling up and down in my direction.

I looked at myself, at what I'd worn to work, the usual jeans and the navy, long-sleeved shirt with the police department logo embroidered on it.

Clearly she thought I'd wear the unexciting outfit to her party. She knew me too well. But I also knew her, knew I wasn't going to get away with it—and had planned ahead. I raised my hands to stop her, as if she were the one who was the law enforcement officer instead of me. "I brought other clothes."

I grabbed my bag and dropped it on her bed. I'd gone to her house directly from work.

"These clothes, were they given to you by the department?" she asked. "If it were in a different size, could a guy wear it?"

I huffed out a laugh as I unzipped the bag. "No. I've been working too many long hours with the Mills murder and the other cases I've got on my plate to think about what to wear. Or do laundry."

"That's fine and all for nine-to-five—"

"Try seven to ten," I corrected.

"Whatever. Are there sequins on what you've brought? Ruffles? Bows? How about a color besides black or navy?"

I swung my gaze her way, gave her a death glare. "Poppy." I never wore sequins or ruffles and she knew it.

She shrugged, making the bright pink angora sweater she wore shift down one shoulder. No one questioned *her* outfits. "I'm just saying, a guy only wants you putting him in handcuffs if you're in bed together."

I pictured that in my mind, getting a guy in

restraints and at my mercy. In bed. The idea was hot, but what melted my butter was the opposite—a guy tying me up and having me at *his* mercy. To allow me to let go, to forget about everything. I wouldn't have to be in charge, wouldn't have to worry if I was doing it right.

That was never going to happen. No way would I be under a guy's control like that. No way would I let a guy take my power from me. I'd done it once, and it had been a nightmare. Worse than that.

Never again. It was safer to be single, to be alone, than to be abused.

"You are insane," I told her.

"You haven't been with a guy since I met you. No dates. Nothing. How long has it been since you've gotten some?" she asked, her perfect arched brow rising.

Far too long since a man-induced orgasm. Well, ever, because I'd had to do it myself during sex. The guys I'd been with couldn't get me there.

"You think a red sweater's going to help me get laid?"

"The police shirt isn't," she countered.

To say we were complete opposites was an understatement. It was a wonder we were friends. I'd met Poppy Nickel in a yoga class at the recreation center when I first moved to town. We'd hit it off, strangely enough. She was petite, curvy and perky. I was tall, far from curvy and surly. She was high maintenance. I considered primping pulling my hair back in a ponytail.

Poppy tried to fix me up with hot guys—without any success—and I kept her out of speeding tickets. Not that she was wild and crazy, but she was definitely more adventurous than me.

And yet she didn't have a man of her own either. For now she was single.

I took the handcuffs from the hook on my belt, dropped them into my bag. "No handcuffs." I pulled out a sweater and held it up between my fingers. "It's a turtleneck, but it's red. Plus I've got a pair of blank skinny jeans to go with it. Will that work?"

She pursed her lips as she considered.

"You're having an outdoor party in December," I reminded her. "It's maybe ten degrees out. There's no way I'm exposing tons of skin. I'll be wearing my coat and hat. Boots. No one's going to see the sweater."

"Fine," she grumbled as she pulled out her cell to check the time. "But keep your hair down. I'm meeting Kit Lancaster, the party planner, at the barn for a final check. I'll be about an hour."

She gave me a little wave, then left me alone to get ready in her huge master suite.

Poppy was rich. It was as simple as that. Her father was Eddie Nickel, the famous movie star. While he spent most of the year in LA or at a film site, his home was in Cutthroat. He had a huge ranch a few miles away from Poppy's place. The town was thrilled he was a resident, bringing the obvious publicity, but also because he'd filmed his last movie here. It had finished up about a month ago, and from what I'd heard, he was remaining in town through the holidays. That last bit I'd learned from a magazine at the checkout counter.

While it didn't have horses or cattle like her dad's property, Poppy's place had tons of land, including a barn and pond where tonight's party was to be held. This wasn't a simple friendly get-together. Poppy had gone all out in her planning with fancy appetizers and drinks, like hot toddies with lots of rum, a live band for dancing on a raised platform, ice skating on a Zamboni-cleared pond. She'd even hired an event planner, Kit Lancaster, who I knew through the Mills investigation.

The party was going to be out under the stars. In December. Her birthday had been last week, so every year she had a combined birthday and holiday party. Over a hundred people were expected.

But not Eddie Nickel, as far as I knew. Poppy didn't talk about her well-known dad all that much. I didn't need to be a detective to know they didn't get along. At all. I'd never met him, never heard of her having lunch with him, going to his house for dinner. Nothing. Because of this, I never brought it up. I could have wheedled the info out of her—it *was* what I did for a living—but I wasn't eager for her to pry into my past either. I'd moved to Cutthroat for a reason, and I wasn't sharing it, even with a girlfriend. She might inspect my party outfits, but she didn't pester me about my past, and for that I was grateful.

I went into the bathroom, stripped out of my clothes, ditching the bland outfit I'd worn to work, and showered.

While I'd never had any issues about being a woman on the Cutthroat police force, I didn't flaunt my femininity much. I didn't want to stand out, not only with my colleagues, but especially with suspects. Outside of work I didn't want to make a huge statement either, going for simple T-shirts and jeans, minimal makeup. It was easy and involved little time in getting ready in the morning, but it also kept me off most men's radars. That worked for me.

I wasn't looking for a guy. I didn't want a relationship. After one total disaster, I was content being alone. It was easier. Safer. So much less dangerous to my body, my mind and my heart.

When I finished my shower, I dried off, dug out clean panties and bra from my bag and put them on, then brushed out my damp hair. Through the closed door, I heard a series of odd thuds. I opened the bathroom door to listen and wondered what Poppy was up to.

"We have to hurry. She's down at the barn and will be back soon."

It was a man's deep voice. Definitely not Poppy. Using the word *we* indicated there were at least two of them. I tiptoed out of the bathroom and onto the second-floor landing, the thick carpet muting any sound I might make. Poppy's house was a new build with large, open rooms in the western style. I was able to see down into the great room from an open balcony and observe a man who'd just climbed through a window.

It wasn't dark out yet, so none of the lights were on. They must have seen Poppy leave and thought the place empty. I'd put my police SUV in her oversize garage so I wouldn't have to scrape ice or snow from it when I left since snow was expected before dawn.

A second man had his head and upper body through the window and was pushing the rest of himself through the opening. He was big and not very nimble.

"She's going to be sorry now," the second guy said, then groaned as he dropped to the wood floor.

Whoever it was didn't like Poppy. The memory of what Mark Knowles had done to Sam Smythe—kidnapping with the intent to rape—was fresh in my mind.

I didn't have my phone with me, but I wasn't letting these two mess with Poppy. No. These guys weren't going to fuck with my friend.

I tiptoed back into Poppy's bedroom, grabbed my gun and handcuffs from my bag, then slowly made my way down the stairs and into the great room.

"Hold it," I said, my voice loud and clear. I had my service weapon raised and pointed at them.

The first guy spun around as the second pushed up from the floor, picking up a cowboy hat that had been beside him and placing it on his head. They stood side by side, their hands automatically going up. Their eyes widened, and they froze in place. Clearly they hadn't expected me. Or my gun.

Now that I could get a good look at them, they

surprised me, too. My detective's eye made out the one on the left as early thirties, six-one, two hundred pounds of lean muscle. Black hair, equally black eyes. No identifying marks or scars that I could see, and he wore a black coat and dark jeans. Black gloves were on his hands, meaning he didn't want to leave fingerprints. The other I pegged as same age, six-four, two fifty. Pure muscle. Light brown hair, closely shaved beard. Green eyes. Flannel shirt and jeans. Cowboy hat.

My woman's eye said, *Holy shit*. They were drop-dead gorgeous. Magazine models but rugged. I doubted they ever set foot in a gym, probably chopped down trees and wrestled moose for exercise.

When I realized I was ogling, I cleared my throat. "You, move two steps to your right." I waved my gun at the dark-haired guy, indicating which way I wanted him to go. He smartly did as I told him.

"Both of you, turn around."

"Whoa, now. I'm all for the right to bear arms, but do you know how to use that thing?"

He did *not* just ask me that. I refused to respond, only glared.

"Don't piss her off," the dark-haired one warned his friend.

"Yeah, don't piss me off."

"You're not going to shoot us in the back, are you?" the bigger guy asked.

"Turn around," I repeated.

They did and I stepped closer. It was hard to decide who to cuff first. I was fairly skilled at self-defense, but they each had eighty or more pounds on me. I assumed it was better to cuff the larger guy first, so I set a hand at the center of his back, his heat radiating into my palm through his flannel. I felt the play of his muscles as he moved, starting to face me. "There's been a—"

I grabbed his right arm at the wrist, bent it at the elbow to bring it behind his back in an arm lock, preventing him from turning around. With his wrist at his spine, I pushed it up toward his head, which would have his shoulder coming out of joint if he didn't bend over. Instinctively he did just that, and I slapped one handcuff on his wrist but kept the arm pinned behind his back.

"Wait a minute!" the other guy said. "There's been a mistake."

I raised my weapon in my free hand and pointed it at Mr. Black Hair, but kept a tight hold on the bigger guy. "Don't move."

Mr. Black Hair froze but smiled, revealing a damned dimple. I blinked, mesmerized by his gorgeousness.

"All right. I won't move. Careful with the gun," he said.

Once again I bristled.

"There's no need for handcuffs," Bigger Guy said, his voice calm as he tried to slowly turn once more. I raised his wrist higher, making him groan at the discomfort.

"On the ground," I told him, my voice just shy of shouting.

At first he wouldn't go, but a little torque on his arm and Bigger Guy dropped to one knee, then the other, his body hitting the hardwood floor like a tree falling in the forest. I sat on his back, straddled him as I grabbed his other wrist and got him cuffed. I spun about on Bigger Guy's back so I faced his feet, aimed the gun at Mr. Black Hair. No way was I taking my eyes off him.

"Don't even think about blinking," I warned.

He lifted his hands a touch higher, slowly shook his head. "No, ma'am."

The front door opened, and Poppy came in, tugging off her winter hat. She made it three steps before she saw us. Her eyes went wide, and her mouth dropped open. "Holy shit."

No one moved for a few seconds; then Poppy burst out laughing. "Oh, this is awesome."

"Pops, tell your gorgeous friend to put her gun away," Mr. Black Hair said.

Poppy held up her hand and kept on laughing. Tears slid down her cheeks. "Oh no. I've got to get my camera."

"Pops!" Mr. Black Hair shouted.

"Fine. Eve, meet my brother, Shane. The guy you're sitting on is Finch."

I glanced up at Mr. Black Hair—Shane. He winked at me. Winked!

"*You're* her brother? Why the hell did you come through the window?" I asked. I felt the cold air pouring in now that my adrenaline was fading. I knew Poppy had a brother, but I'd never met him before. Poppy wasn't one for family photos about her house, and I had never known what he looked like. Until now.

"What was it going to be this time?" Poppy asked. "Ping-Pong balls in my bathroom? Plastic wrap the toilet seats? Ice cubes filling the fridge? Shampoo in the washing machine?"

"Nothing bad," Shane said. "Only two hundred balloons in your bedroom."

I saw the small helium tank on the floor by the window, most likely the first thump I'd heard when I was in the bathroom. Shane had to have been the second.

I climbed off Finch, put my hands on my hips. "You're here to *prank*? Can't you do that by using the door?"

Shane shrugged, then grinned. "We couldn't risk setting off the alarm."

That made complete sense. Sneak in through your sister's window.

"It's a birthday thing," he added, as if that explained it all. "Mine's in June, and this year Poppy put hundreds of caterpillars in my truck. I couldn't find them all before they turned, and I had butterflies in there for a week."

"That was a good one," Poppy said. "I wondered when you were going to attack. Totally backfired though. Suckers."

"Um, I'm the one handcuffed and on the floor," Finch prompted.

"Oh, um... the keys are in my bag upstairs," I said, flustered, looking down at the big, brawny cowboy sprawled on the floor. His hat had been knocked off.

"I'll get them," Poppy offered, still laughing as she went up the steps.

"Yeah, there's no place for you to keep them in that outfit," Shane murmured, his gaze raking over every inch of me.

I looked down at myself, realized what I was wearing. What I *wasn't* wearing. Clothes. I had on a red bra and panty set and that was it.

I squeaked in utter embarrassment.

I'd gone into police mode and forgotten everything, including the fact that I was practically naked. Before I could panic or even grab a blanket off the back of the sofa, Poppy hurried down the stairs and tossed me the keys.

Her cell rang and she raced off to get it, quickly getting into a conversation about fairy lights and generators, so I assumed it was Kit.

I knelt beside Finch and opened the cuffs, keeping them once he was free. "Sorry about that."

He pushed himself up so he was seated on the floor and we were eye to eye. Grabbing his hat, he set it on his head. He smiled, his green eyes raking over my face, then lower. "I'm not sorry. I had a pretty woman straddling me." He leaned in close, lowered his voice. "I liked it when you were on top."

I blushed to the roots of my hair at what he meant.

"I… um… need to find some clothes."

Finch shook his head. "You don't have to for our sakes."

"That's right. The view's pretty damned fine," Shane said, going to the window and shutting it. "I'm guessing you're Eve Miranski, the detective. We've heard about you. I figured we'd meet someday, but not like this."

Finch stood and I had to tilt my head back to look at both of them. Now that they weren't sociopaths intent on doing Poppy bodily harm, I could appreciate how hot they were. How their clothes clung to their strong physiques. Their square jaws. Intense gazes. Big hands.

And I was still in my underwear. I started walking backward toward the stairs, my gun in one hand—lowered now—and handcuffs in the other. Now that they weren't being held at gunpoint, their bodies were relaxed and their gazes wandered. I couldn't miss the heat in their eyes. I also couldn't miss one very obvious thing. No, *two*. They were both hard.

And big.

Big and hard.

My mouth was dry. "Okay, so… this has been interesting. Sorry to have, um, messed up your prank. I guess you'll have to come up with a different one." I stumbled around an end table. "I'll... um... see you later."

They watched me go, and I felt their gazes on every inch of my skin.

"Definitely," Shane said.

"At the party." Finch tipped his chin up. "You can ditch the gun but bring the handcuffs."

2

$\mathcal{S}$HANE

"I HOPE you have on that red lingerie beneath all those layers."

It had been three hours since the takedown in Poppy's great room, and we'd finally cornered Eve at the party, since she was doing her blatant best to avoid us.

We hadn't pulled off the birthday prank, but that wasn't new. Sometimes it took a few attempts to accomplish. Every year it was hilarious to see her reaction. Poppy and I had been at it, messing with each other, for years. It was one of the ways we'd found humor in growing up in the Nickel household. It hadn't been the posh lifestyle the gossip magazines painted it to be. Eddie Nickel wasn't the loving father. He didn't know what love was, only humiliation, shame and beatings.

After I started hanging out with Finch in high school, he'd joined in the fun on occasion, especially when I needed an extra set of hands or to work quickly, like tonight and the plan to inflate two hundred balloons before Poppy returned home.

Poppy and I were adults, but we wouldn't stop pranking each other. It was too much fun. Eddie Nickel might pop into Cutthroat from time to time, telling the media he wanted some *family time,* like now, over the holidays. That was a complete joke. Poppy and I were all each other had.

But today? This specific prank? I didn't care that we'd failed. Hell, no. What guy would want to miss being stopped by a gorgeous, gun-toting female in her underwear? Not any who had a pulse.

I'd been hard since the first moment I laid eyes on her, and I hadn't been the one to be straddled. Fuck, her legs had been spread wide around Finch's broad back, her hot pussy pressing against him. It had been ball aching just to witness, and I was jealous of him— even if he'd been handcuffed.

"I hope you like getting your throat punched if you keep talking like that," Eve countered before taking a sip of the hot rum punch. She wore jeans and heavy winter boots and a thick down jacket. A yellow hat covered her head. She looked... soft, but her words were all sharp wit.

"Ouch," Finch commented, running a hand over his beard and grinning.

Eve had made herself scarce after the... incident. Until now. She shouldn't feel embarrassed about what had happened. I'd been impressed by her skill. Her levelheadedness. We wanted to put her at ease, but it seemed she used sarcasm as a defense mechanism, and that made her... prickly.

I understood that well enough, employing any means of self-preservation growing up. Poppy and I hated our dad the same amount, although I held an extra bit of rage and hatred for him for how he'd hurt her. I'd tried to protect her as much as I could, but we'd been kids and Eddie Nickel... well, he'd been an asshole cloaked beneath America's hottest Hollywood star. I'd even stayed in town instead of going away to college, letting Poppy live with me while she finished high school. No fucking way could I have left her alone in that house.

I refused to use a dime of his wealth. To spite him,

I avoided the limelight, going so far as to work for the forest service where I spent most of my time alone in the woods. I owned a house in town—a small one completely unlike the Nickel ranch—but I lived most of the year in a small cabin on national forest land. I liked the quiet. The solitude. The lack of hype, paparazzi.

Poppy did the opposite. She spited our old man by using his cash he'd put in trust funds for us when we were born. She'd earned it, she said. Since he'd beaten and verbally abused us until I was big enough to defend us both, I couldn't agree more. She wasn't shallow, though, wasting her life on frivolous shit. She'd gone to college and was a social worker at the local middle school, helping to ensure kids had access to help we'd never had.

Poppy'd bought a big spread with the money and used it to throw big parties like this one. The barn doors were open wide, the tables of food just inside. A raised dance floor had been placed beneath rows of strung lights. A band was off to the side. The pond was frozen solid, cleared of snow, and people were skating. Benches had been placed along the edge for people to sit and switch out of their shoes.

I guessed at least seventy-five people were here, and I knew almost all of them. But there was only one

I was interested in. The *very* sexy Eve Miranski. And we finally had her in front of us.

"I've made it years without meeting either of you," she snapped. "Now I can't make it two hours."

I grinned, lifted a hand to brush her long hair off her shoulder. The tresses were silky and soft to the touch, and I wondered if the rest of her felt the same way. We'd seen practically every inch of her, knew she was tall and lean, muscular and fit. She didn't have tons of curves, but what she did have was taut, toned and perfect. Sadly all of that was covered against the cold with a heavy coat and hat. If I could have superpowers, it would be X-ray vision.

Her eyes were dark and fringed with the longest lashes. She wore only a hint of makeup, and her lips were shiny and glossy. Her mouth was fucking kissable, although I had to wonder if I'd have my knee kicked out and shoved face-first into the snow if I tried.

It would be well worth it.

"We're that likable," I told her.

She rolled her eyes.

"Are you two always together? Like Laurel and Hardy?" she wondered.

"More like Fred Flintstone and Barney Rubble," Finch countered. I would have thought Butch Cassidy and the Sundance Kid, but I didn't mind being Fred Flintstone. We had looked like bumbling fools earlier. If the Stone Age shoes fit...

"As for always together?" I asked. "With you we are."

She glanced between us as if she were watching a tennis match. "Together? Are... um... you serious?"

I glanced at Finch, then nodded. "Fuck yeah, we're serious."

We wanted Eve, not only because she looked pretty damned incredible in her underwear, but she was feisty, didn't hold back on anything and was prepared to throat punch both of us. She was intriguing. Sexy. Smart. A little wild. Definitely dangerous. Prickly as fuck.

I wanted to get her between us, loosen her up with a few orgasms. Make her forget everything but our names. Like her fellow detective, Nix, we wanted to share a woman, and we were making that very clear.

"You don't even know me."

"That's different than us wanting you," I said. "What we're saying is we *both* want to get to know you."

Finch set his hand on her shoulder, very slowly, very gently. We didn't hurt women. Ever. That was why we hadn't resisted at all earlier. Besides her pointing a gun at us. With his size, Finch could have easily overpowered her, gun or not.

She wasn't like any other woman we'd ever met. It didn't matter that she knew how to incapacitate a guy or get him in handcuffs. We treated women with care. And this one? Eve Miranski? We would handle her gently, not like a delicate flower but like we would a bomb.

"It would be easier to get to know you if you didn't try to hide from us, sugar," Finch said, his hand still on her shoulder.

Her eyes flared with anger. I wasn't sure if it was from the endearment or the statement. "I haven't been hiding from you."

We pinned her with hard stares. She squirmed.

She looked down at her feet, then back at us. "Fine, I've been hiding from you."

"Is it because we saw you in pretty red panties and bra? Trust us, there's nothing to be embarrassed about."

Even under the fairy lights, I could see her blush.

"I avoid situations like this," she says, circling her finger in the air between us.

Finch frowned, leaned down so they were eye level. "What do you mean?"

Her gaze flicked between us again.

"We didn't hurt you, did we?" I asked, and Finch tensed beside me.

She frowned. "What? No."

"Then what—"

"Men. I hide from men."

"You sure as hell didn't hide from us, sugar," Finch said with a smile.

She pursed her lips. "That's exactly it. I didn't do... earlier intentionally. You guys broke into Poppy's house, and I'm a law enforcement officer. I don't flaunt my body to men. Look at me." Her head dropped. "I'm not giving off signals. I'm not flirting. I look like the Stay Puft Marshmallow Man in this coat. I'm not interested, whatever you're offering."

"You're not gay," I stated.

She closed her eyes. Huffed. "Jesus, if a woman isn't interested, it doesn't mean she's a lesbian."

True enough. There were lots of women that didn't do it for me. It didn't make me into guys. It made me selective. "You just don't like us."

She tucked her chin into the high collar of her coat. It was fucking freezing out here and I knew just the way to warm her up—and it wasn't more hot rum punch.

"Actually I don't really like any guys right about now. I'm not interested in starting anything."

"You're not interested in sex?" Finch asked, his gaze raking her over. He let his hand fall away from her shoulder.

A waiter came by with a trayful of finger foods. He'd heard Finch's question and glanced at Eve. Even though she blushed, she gave the guy a death glare and he fled.

"I like sex just fine," she replied. "Especially when it's me and my battery-operated boyfriend," she added.

I put my hand on my chest. "Oh, that's harsh. Now I'm picturing you in bed, in only your red lingerie, legs parted."

Her mouth fell open at my bold words. I leaned in, breathed in the scent of rum and fruity shampoo.

"Your fingers are tugging that scrap of red silk to the side so you can run a big dildo up and down to get nice and wet. Then you fuck yourself with it."

Finch made a rumbling sound. Yeah, he could envision that, too.

"When you say you're not interested in guys *right about now,* how long has it been?" Finch asked.

She took a big swig of her hot drink. I knew a stall tactic when I saw one. "A while," she replied neutrally.

I liked the idea of no guy getting his hands—or dick—on her, seeing what we'd seen of her earlier, but she was a passionate woman and deserved sexual pleasure. It was a shame she denied herself.

"You're an up-front woman," I continued. "You don't like games, I can tell. I'll state it plainly then. We want you, Eve."

"That's right," Finch said. "We want to get to *know* you. Some guy obviously hurt you. We won't."

Her back went as stiff as board. Yeah, someone had messed with her. "You won't hurt me? Really." She sounded more sarcastic than reassured.

"We didn't earlier," Finch reminded her.

"I was holding a gun."

"Think that would have stopped us if we really wanted to do you harm?" I asked.

She studied us. "I can take care of myself."

"You sure as fuck can," Finch said without blinking. And she hadn't even been dressed. "I remember how hot your pussy was against my back. You can tackle me anytime you want."

"We won't hurt you," I repeated, patting my chest. "Here." I was getting an idea of why she was so jaded. Some guy had fucked with her. Hurt her enough to put her off men entirely.

"You can't say that," she countered, shaking her head. "A relationship only leads to heartache and worse."

Yeah, I'd been dead-on. I didn't know who it was that had done a number on her, but if I ever found out, the asshole was going six feet under.

"Fine. No relationship. Use us for our bodies," Finch offered.

What the fuck was he saying? We wanted it all with Eve—or at least to see where this could go. Not a one-night stand. No fucking way. That wouldn't be enough.

What was he playing at?

She laughed, then quickly stopped. "You're serious."

Finch shrugged. "Guys use women all the time. Use us. Ditch the vibrator and go for the real thing. Times two. Trust me, we'll make you come. Hard."

I was slow. Thank fuck Finch wasn't. We wanted more out of Eve. Sure, we'd had flings. Solo and together. If I had to come up with one of those women's names, I couldn't. Nor picture their faces in my mind. That was pretty shitty, but I'd never led one of them wrong and they probably didn't remember much about me either. As for those who'd just wanted to fuck Eddie Nickel's son... I'd caught on to that back in college.

I wanted Eve. For more than her body, but we could start with no-strings sex. If that was how she wanted to play it, to keep her heart out of it for now, that worked. Once we were in her bed, we could take our time, show her how real men treated a lady. To prove that we wouldn't hurt her. That we were playing for keeps.

"We'll be here, sugar," Finch said. "Just say the word and we'll take care of you."

3

VE

WHAT THE HELL had that been about? Finch and Shane had offered me—point-blank—a no-strings fling... with both of them. Sex. As much as I wanted. Orgasms, as much as I wanted as well. The question was, why?

I'd practically ripped Finch's arm out of his socket, forced him to the floor and handcuffed him. I'd pointed a gun at Shane. It wasn't the best first impression, that was for sure. They weren't mad. They were... amused. I somehow intrigued them, which was completely ridiculous.

They intrigued me, that was for damned sure. I couldn't believe I never knew Poppy's brother was such a hottie. And Finch, well, when God handed out the good genes, he'd certainly shown up.

They weren't hard on the eyes. Far from it. It had been an hour since they'd left me standing by the barn, speechless and confused. And horny. Since then I'd counted five women who'd come up to Shane by the bar, and two had given their phone number to Finch. I hadn't even known in the day of cell phones that the concept of writing it on a little slip of paper was still a thing.

They weren't hard up. They'd said they were *hard,* for me. Again, why? Why me?

I hadn't been playing hard to get. I hadn't been playing at all. Why not go for the blonde in the pink puffy coat or the brunette in the *very* snug black ski pants? They'd seen me in my underwear, knew that I had as many curves as a straight line.

They'd not only offered themselves up for sexual services, but had walked away. They were letting *me* decide the if or when.

"Earth to Eve."

I blinked, realizing I'd zoned out on Nix. He and his girlfriend, Kit, had caught up to me by the bar. I couldn't blame my behavior on the rum drinks even though I'd had three. I blamed it on two hot cowboys.

"Sorry." I offered him a small smile. "What were you saying?"

"The mayor called after you left the station."

I groaned, rolled my eyes. We'd been feeling the pressure from his office ever since Erin Mills had been murdered in the fall. Who had we interviewed? What new evidence was there? What had we discovered?

"He wants resolution we can't give him. Not without a break in the case," I reminded him.

Nix knew the score. He was my partner, the only other detective on the Cutthroat Police Department. We were handling the Mills case plus our regular workload.

Kit took Nix's hand, looked up at him. "I thought we weren't going to talk about work tonight." She'd been Erin Mills's roommate and had found the body. She wanted to see the killer caught as well, but she was right, it was a party, not work hours.

Donovan Nash, who formerly worked in the DA's office, joined us, handing Kit a mug that had steam rising from the top.

"Hey, Eve."

"We were just talking about your dad," I said.

I knew Nix really well since we worked together

forty-plus hours a week. Because of that, I was friendly with Kit, although they'd only started dating right after Erin Mills was murdered. I'd also worked with Donovan, but only in the courtroom when I had to give testimony on a case he tried.

He'd quit the DA's office and was going solo now. I envied him the freedom from office politics, although he didn't get too much escape since his father was the mayor.

Donovan held up his hands. "I'm sure his constituents want a murderer behind bars. Not that we don't," he added when he knew Nix and I would bite his head off.

"Since you left the station before I did, you missed the memo. Meeting tomorrow, eleven o'clock."

"On a Saturday?" Kit asked. "Never mind, I know. There's a killer out there."

Just talking about it made me tense. The stress was starting to give me heartburn, and I slept like crap. We had no new leads, no compelling evidence that pointed us in any specific direction. The killer was someone who'd known Erin. There hadn't been a break-in at her house. A fight had gone bad. But who?

We'd learned that Erin had been an active dater. I wasn't going to judge any woman for sleeping with a number of men. She'd been an adult, single, and it was her own prerogative. Because of that, it was almost impossible to narrow the suspect list. Was it a jealous ex-lover? A random guy she met at a bar and took home? Had she been stalked? Did she cut someone off while driving and they followed her?

These were the questions Nix and I asked ourselves every day because there were no answers.

A waiter came by with a tray loaded with hot drinks. Nix stopped him, handed one to me, kept one for himself. "Tonight we have fun. Tomorrow we deal with the mayor."

He clinked his glass with mine.

"The party's a hit. Your work is done. What should we do?" he asked Kit.

"Ice skate," she replied almost gleefully.

"Come on, Kitty Kat. Show me what you've got." Donovan wrapped an arm around Kit and led her toward the frozen pond, offering us a little wave as goodbye.

"You okay?" Nix asked me, studying my face.

I was tall, five-nine, but I still had to tip my head back to look at him. I nodded.

He angled his head toward the benches where Donovan and Kit sat to put on skates. "You good on your own if I catch up with them?"

I loved that he and Donovan were dating Kit

together. They knew their minds, didn't give a shit about what anyone thought and went for it. Kit looked like a *very* happy woman, and I envied her.

That made me think of Shane and Finch. I didn't want a relationship, not anything like the solid one Nix was building with Donovan and Kit. It didn't mean I couldn't have that smile on my face like Kit's, which looked like she had been well fucked, and recently. And often.

I didn't need a relationship. I looked out toward the pond, saw Shane and Finch talking with Poppy. They'd offered.

All I had to do was accept.

I looked to Nix. "I'm fine. Go. Have fun."

"You, too."

"I plan to," I murmured after he walked off. I'd been hot for two cowboys for hours, ever since I pointed my gun at them in Poppy's living room. Shane's dirty talk... God, that had been hot. It had made my nipples hard, my panties wet. I wanted what they offered. Why shouldn't I take it? No strings. Only orgasms. It was insane, but... yes, please.

I walked over to join Shane, Finch and Poppy. "Hey! Having fun?" she asked.

"Great party," I said, glancing around. The band was playing. People were dancing. Skating. Drinking.

"Thanks." Someone shouted Poppy's name, and we looked toward the dance floor. A small group waved her over.

"Gotta run!"

She dashed off, leaving me with Shane and Finch.

"I accept your offer," I blurted out before I could change my mind.

Finch's hand froze, the beer he was drinking halfway to his mouth. "Sugar," he murmured, and I watched as his gaze heated. He handed the beer to a passing waiter without looking away from me.

Shane took a step closer, tucked my hair back over my shoulder. I shivered even though I wasn't cold at all.

"I want to sample the goods first," I said.

"What?" Shane asked, a crease forming in his brow.

I shrugged. "You said no relationship, so you're offering a service of sorts. I want to know I'll be satisfied."

"That's right. You don't have to buy the whole cow. You'll get the milk for free."

My mouth fell open at Shane's words. Processed, then rolled my eyes. "Wrong analogy. A woman has no interest in buying the whole pig when all she wants is a little sausage."

Shane's deep laugh had people turning to look our way. "Fine," he replied. "Only the sausage."

"And they're not little," Finch added with a wink.

"I still want a sample first." I shrugged, tried to sound casual. "I mean, a woman's got to know if a man's worth taking to bed."

Finch grinned. "Challenge accepted."

Shane took my hand, led me around the side of the barn. "You don't have to worry your pretty little head about that."

"Wait, where are we going?" I asked as the glow from the fairy lights disappeared, the sounds from the party faded. We were alone.

Finch was right behind us.

"You want a sample, we'll give you a sample." Shane moved in, pressed me against the wall. Kissed me.

Holy shit, could he kiss. A big hand cupped my cheek and held my head right where he wanted me. I moaned when he nipped my lower lip, then angled us so he could go deep, his tongue tangling with mine. My nipples hardened. My core ached to be filled. My body went soft, pliant, and between the barn at my back and the hard press of his body against my front, I remained upright.

The temperature hovered well below freezing and

I should have been a block of ice standing outside away from the heat lamps, but I was burning up. I was surprised the snow at our feet didn't melt. The zipper on my thick down jacket slid all the way down. His lips brushed along my jaw to my ear.

"Fuck, you taste so good. Are you this sweet everywhere?" Shane asked.

I whimpered at his question. His tongue flicked the *very* sensitive spot behind my ear, then moved down the side of my neck.

I gripped his coat, held on for dear life.

"This is crazy," I said, my eyes opening to look up at the sea of stars across the inky-black sky. My breath came out in little clouds of steam.

"Not crazy. Perfect. You wanted a sample, sugar." Finch stood directly beside me. His warm hand slid under my sweater, over the bare skin of my belly to cup my small breast. "Fuck, you're so soft."

I could barely see his face—the bright moonlight was shielded by the wide brim of his cowboy hat—as his other hand joined the first beneath my clothes and played with my nipples through my bra. My back arched instinctively into his calloused palms.

"I... wow, this is intense. Maybe we should talk some more?" I asked. I'd never felt like this. So hot, so needy. So quickly. I was out of control. Hell, I had *no* control over my body, how they were making me feel. Both of them.

I was making out with two guys, and that was why this was insane.

I was crazy. I didn't go to parties, drink, make out with strangers. *Hot* strangers. This was so unlike me, telling two guys I wanted no-strings sex. Wanted a sample.

Okay, I'd kissed guys before, but one guy at a time. And it had been a long time. Loooonnnnnggg. My self-imposed ban on men had held for years. Until now, until Poppy's party. Until them.

The asshole I'd been with in the past hadn't gotten me this hot in all the time we'd been together. Looking back—because I hadn't recognized it at the time—it was the demeaning and cruel words that had never gotten me wet, and no wonder. I hadn't been loved. I hadn't even been lusted after. I'd been a "thing," and I'd been made to feel worthless.

These two? I felt desired. Wanted. Safe. Finch and Shane were already to second base, and I could probably come if they kept it up.

I blamed this insanity on the hot rum flowing through my veins. On Poppy. On my desperate need for a break from the Mills murder case that had taken up all my time and brain power. Poppy had wanted me to have a night off, to forget about everything, even for a little while.

I was definitely doing that with two handsome cowboys. One dark, the other darker. One tall, the other broader. Both gorgeous. Virile. Manly. I was here willingly with them in this secluded spot. I'd asked for it. I'd wanted this, but God, it was hard to give in, to let go. My brain and my libido were at odds.

"You want to talk?" Finch murmured. "Sugar, we can talk all you want. Should we chat about politics?"

Shane huffed out a laugh but didn't stop licking and nibbling at my neck.

"God, no," I practically moaned, then angled my head to give Shane better access.

"You want to talk about how responsive you are?" Finch gave my breasts a gentle squeeze. "I want a turn with her mouth."

I laughed at that. Finch, who was the size of a Viking, sounded like a toddler not getting his fair share with a toy.

Shane growled against my collarbone. "You're feeling her up and you want her mouth, too?" That was a sound of possession, and it sent a thrill through me. He didn't want to give me up.

"Fine. She's got other places to kiss." The cowboy dropped to his knees in the snow. His big body pushed the other guy to the side, but Shane didn't stop kissing me. "Don't you, sugar?"

Finch's hands went to my jeans, opening them and pushing them over my hips, taking my panties with them. My breasts tingled and I wanted my nipples tugged some more, suddenly lonely without his hands on me. The freezing air rushed over the bared skin of my hips, butt and wet center.

"Oh my God," I breathed, glancing down. Finch took off his hat, set it beside him as he looked up at me. His eyes were dark, and I couldn't miss the desire I saw there. He wanted me.

Shane lifted his head from my neck, his breath fanning against my damp skin. "You wanted a sample of what it would be like. Want him to eat your pussy?" he murmured. "Or did you get enough? We can go back to the party and talk, leaving you all wet and needy."

I nodded, then shook my head, confused as to how to answer. Did I want a big, brawny cowboy to put his mouth on me and make me come?

Yes. Yes, I did.

Did I care that he was practically a stranger? Did I care I'd only talked and flirted with them for the past thirty minutes? That I'd forced him to Poppy's floor and handcuffed him?

No, I didn't care. My pussy didn't care. I had no doubt he knew what he was doing, that I was going to get the most *epic* sample of his prowess. That he could give me the first man-induced orgasm I'd had in years.

Standing behind a barn.

I looked around but saw only darkness. I heard the soft sound of music coming from the party, the murmur of voices. A glow came around the corner from the strings of fairy lights. Anyone could find us. "Please don't stop," I told him.

Finch grinned. "Step nice and wide so I can get in there."

I did as he said, although with my jeans around my thighs, I couldn't move too far.

He took a deep breath. "Fuck, you even smell sweet. If you still feel like talking, you can tell me how you like it."

I should have been embarrassed by their dirty talk, but I wasn't. I was turned on. Wildly.

"I... it's been a long time. I don't know." My breath escaped in hot little pants.

I could see his wicked grin. "Just grab hold of my hair, sugar, and I'll figure out what you like when you start tugging." He didn't wait a second longer. Leaning forward, he licked up my seam. I gasped and did as he said, tangling my fingers in the soft strands. "You're dripping wet. You love this, don't you?"

I could deny it, but he knew the truth. They both did. I could barely focus as the cowboy ate me out with a diligence that was impressive. Tongue, lips, the graze of teeth, even fingers got into the action.

Shane tipped my chin to look at him, and I got lost in his black gaze. "I love your little sounds of pleasure, but I'm not sharing you with anyone but Finch." He covered my mouth with his, swallowing all the gasps and moans.

Finch. The guy whose tongue was flicking across my clit. Whose finger was curling over my G-spot, which I hadn't even known I had. It was like he'd hit a button that had me close to coming.

Two men. I'd never had such an assault on my senses. Four hands. Two mouths. And they still had their clothes on.

I had no idea I was so easy to arouse, but I came ridiculously quickly, ridiculously hard, my hands in Finch's hair, holding him in place, my hips rocking into him as I reveled in the most incredible pleasure. Ever.

Shane kissed me, swallowing my cries.

"Fuck, that was hot," Finch said as he kissed my thigh. "Sugar, you can let go of my hair now."

My fingers unclenched, and I laughed as Finch stood. "Sorry."

"Nothing to be sorry about." He wiped his mouth with the back of his hand, and I could see my arousal glisten on his lips and beard. The two of them worked my panties and jeans back into place.

Someone came around the barn, breaking the spell between us. All we could make out was the guy's silhouette against the party lights, but he paused when he saw us, mumbled an apology and turned around.

It was enough to make me realize I was getting chilled, that the rum had worn off some. Holy shit, that had been some sample.

What would it be like if we were actually indoors, in a bed? Naked? That while I'd had the best orgasm of my life, I realized how insane it was. Crazy.

There was that word again.

"We should get back to the party. It's too cold to take things further," Shane said, tucking my hair back over my shoulder. I wore a knit hat, but I had left my hair long.

"I want a bed for what I want to do to you," Finch added, taking hold of my hand and kissing the knuckles. "If you liked the sample, that is." His grin was of self-satisfaction, knowing his oral skills were incredible.

As we came around the old barn and rejoined the party, I worried everyone was staring at me, that they could tell what we'd done. Ridiculous, unless they'd heard me come. No, impossible, or at least I hoped.

I did a quick scan. Poppy was dancing. Nix and Kit were with Donovan skating.

It was obvious how tight they were, how in love. I'd never said a word about any relationships with him. Being cops and partners, we were close, but not *that* close. Besides, I didn't have any kind of love life to share. I still didn't because what Shane and Finch had done to me wasn't love. It was sex. *Almost* sex. A *sample*. I'd made it clear I wasn't looking for a relationship, and they were fine with that. Hell, they'd offered themselves to me.

And had certainly done so. I'd gotten off. They hadn't.

I wasn't a prude. Obviously I was fine with my sexuality if I let two guys have their way with me, but it wasn't *me*. I hadn't slept with a man in years. Four, to be exact. And not just sex. Kissing. Making out. Whatever we'd done behind the barn. I'd been man-free all this time. One party and a little liquor and I was close to changing that.

From what I could tell, Shane and Finch were nice guys. While Shane was Poppy's brother, they seemed to really get along, to have a close relationship. She seemed to like Finch, too. I had no doubt she'd give us getting together two thumbs-up. Still, nice or not, I didn't want a relationship—not that I thought an orgasm constituted one—on top of everything else right now. Murder and multiple men in my life didn't mix.

"I... I should go." I'd gone a little wild. Forgotten about work. About the case. About steering clear of men. Even though my body hummed and my muscles felt like pulled taffy, I had to keep my head on straight. One incredible orgasm and I was considering *more.*

Shane and Finch turned to face me, to block out the party with their big bodies. "What? Now?" Finch asked.

I could see him clearly. The light brown hair that peeked out beneath his cowboy hat. The tanned skin, the strong jaw that was covered in a closely shaved beard. The concern and lingering heat in his eyes. I tilted my head back to meet his eyes.

"This isn't me," I practically pleaded. "I don't tell guys I'll go for a no-strings fling."

Shane and Finch glanced at each other, then back at me. "This *is* you," Finch said.

I pushed at him because I wasn't going to be

patronized, but they wouldn't let me by. They didn't know me, know what was in my head.

"With *us*, you're like this. Hot, responsive," he added.

"It's fucking incredible that we could see you like that, that you trusted us enough to give in to what's between us," Shane said.

Had I? Had I given in, submitted? Handed over every thought and worry to them?

I had. *Shit.*

"There's nothing between us," I countered. "I told you, there can't be."

"There can, if you let it," Shane added.

I studied them. They were so handsome. So... nice. And sexually skilled beyond anything I'd ever experienced, and they hadn't even gotten naked.

"Why?" I asked. All of a sudden I remembered how it had felt with Chad, my asshole ex. The feelings of inadequacy. Of shame. Of feeling less.

"Why what?" Finch asked, running a hand over his beard.

"Why do you want me so much? Is it because you didn't get off?" I asked, glancing down at the fronts of their jeans. We were back under the strings of fairy lights, and I couldn't miss the thick outlines of their dicks straining against the material.

A couple walked past, and Shane waited to respond until they were out of earshot. He took a half step closer. "Don't insult us or yourself. We want you because you're smart. Funny. Hot as hell. Sexy."

"You got all that from the, what, the half hour we talked?" I was lying to myself. I'd learned a lot about *them* in that amount of time. I wouldn't have gone off with them otherwise.

Both shrugged.

"You come like a dream," Shane said.

"When you know, you know," Finch added.

When you know, you know.

My heart thudded at those words because they were dead-on. Shit. I felt different with them, like I was everything they said. That I was more than my badge, that I wasn't just a woman to fuck. They intrigued me. They made me hot. Hell, they'd made me come, and that scared me. *They* scared me.

Yeah, I was afraid of how they made me feel, but I'd learned it was safer for my heart to keep men at a distance, not on their knees with their faces between my thighs.

I'd been stupid thinking I could do simple. It was what I wanted, but I couldn't pull it off. One orgasm didn't mean forever. It couldn't.

"I told you no strings. I can't have more. All *I* know is... is, I have to go."

This time, when I tried to get past, they let me. I tracked down Poppy and said goodbye, then fled. From feeling, because it hurt too much. Alone was better than broken.

4

 INCH

"WE SHOULDN'T HAVE LET her go like that," I said, keeping my eyes on the road.

It had started snowing before dawn and hadn't let up since. At least six inches had fallen, and another foot was expected before the front moved on. The roads, at least this far out of town, had not been cleared. I didn't give a shit because my truck was huge and had a plow on the front. With my driveway being a half mile long and it snowing all the fucking time, I used it frequently.

"We didn't have much choice. I didn't see any

handcuffs on her, but I wouldn't put it past her to have arrested us," Shane muttered.

There had been no point in staying at the party after Eve left, so we'd both gone home. Me, with a taste of her pussy on my tongue and a raging hard-on that wouldn't go down, even after I rubbed one out in the shower.

"You could have asked Poppy more about her."

He turned, glared at me. "This isn't middle school. I'm not going to ask Poppy about a girl we think is cute. The one thing my sister and I don't do is talk about our sex lives. If I discover she's not a virgin, I'll have to go kill some guys."

"She's twenty-four. She's not a virgin," I said, slowly shaking my head.

"She'll be a virgin when she's sixty and a grandmother," Shane shot back, making me grin. "Forget about Poppy. I want to talk about Eve."

"Fine. Eve. The hot detective. You said she was cute? *Cute?* She could flay us alive with that smart tongue of hers. She's hot as fuck and that pussy..." My mouth watered at the thought of getting between her thighs again.

Shane groaned. "All I got to do was kiss her. You got your hands on those tits and your mouth on her pussy."

"I finger fucked her, too." My dick hardened remembering how wet she'd been. How tight. How she'd rippled around my finger when she came.

"Fuck you."

I couldn't help messing with him. "I'd rather fuck *her*."

I slowed and carefully steered the truck onto the county road that led south toward my ranch. Since Shane couldn't leave his forest service vehicle at my house for his days off, I'd picked him up at his cabin. We were headed back to my ranch to collect our snowmobiles, which I kept stored in one of my outbuildings. Our plan was to park at a trail access Lucas Mills had told us about and spend the day in the backcountry. The new snow would make for a great ride.

"She was incredible," he said. "We have to persuade her to have more than a fling. I want her and not as a quick lay."

"I only suggested a no-strings relationship because she was scared of more."

"To make her change her mind through multiple orgasms."

"Exactly," I replied.

"The only way that's going to happen is to get her between us again."

Sure, I wanted to get more than my finger in her pussy, but I wanted to know *her*. "I shouldn't push for more. I'm not a good bet and you know it."

His head flopped back against the headrest. "Not this again," he groaned. "Jesus, you're too hard on yourself. She was into us. *Us*. Hell, she was into your mouth on her pussy. Not me, not me and a sidekick. Me. You."

"Whatever. Figures the woman both my dick and my heart wants is a fucking detective. What are the chances of that?"

I'd gone to jail for assault. I'd beat up an asshole who'd been slapping a friend of ours around, and I didn't stand for that shit. Not when I'd been nineteen, not now. But beating the shit out of a Cutthroat Richie Rich, regardless of the fact that he'd been assaulting a woman, meant I'd gone to jail.

No woman wanted to be with a guy who hit, regardless of *who* or *why* I'd done so. It had been ten years since I'd gotten out, and while a woman might like to fuck a convict, that was as far as it went. Especially not a police officer.

I wasn't too keen on being taken to the ground and handcuffed. If it had been anyone besides a hot, scantily clad woman, I'd have probably panicked. But feeling her thighs squeeze my sides, the heat from her pussy against my lower back, had made me forget everything but how hard she made my dick.

Clearly Eve didn't know my past, or she'd have kept me in those fucking handcuffs.

No one wanted the long haul with me. The white picket fence and two-point-five kids and a dog. My property was too big for the fence, but the right woman would get a ranch and a dog. And me. And Shane. Hopefully she'd give us a bunch of kids.

"You're the one she spread her legs for," he prompted. "You're the one she wanted."

I glanced at Shane and gave him snark. "Sure, pretty boy."

Shane was the guy all the women went after. Dark hair, piercing eyes. Muscles. A quick wit and a quicker grin. Plus he had a movie-star dad, even though the guy was a total fucker. On the surface, that combination was lethal to a woman's panties.

"Don't forget, besides being the *pretty boy,* I'm rich, too. You're not the only man who's single," he countered. "None have wanted me either, at least for more than a quick fuck. So calm your tits."

I sighed. He was right. I wasn't the only single guy in Cutthroat. At least I knew where I stood with women. Shane probably had to figure out if his dick was getting sucked because a woman actually wanted to satisfy Shane himself or because she got on her knees to get closer to his father.

"If she's the one for us, she'll see me for *me,* not for the fact that I'm Eddie Nickel's son. She'll see you for more than just your record. She'll understand why. She won't give a shit. Hell, she'll think you're fucking honorable."

I shot him a doubtful look. Eve might only want sex, but I doubted she wanted to take a felon's dick for a ride.

———

EVE

"I WANT to know why the killer hasn't been caught. So do Keith and Ellen Mills."

Anthony Nash, better known as Mayor Nash, stood before our desks, arms crossed over his chest. I pegged him to be in his late fifties, early sixties with salt-and-pepper hair. He was six feet tall, but his ego was much bigger. I doubted he cared that justice was served for Erin Mills as much as the case being closed so he wasn't known as the mayor who let a murderer roam free.

"It's one man," he continued. "There are only so many people in Cutthroat. About half of them are women."

Each officer had a desk in the large room. Nix and I were the only detectives on the department, and ours were in the corner by the windows. While the mayor scolded us like high schoolers caught out after curfew, the rest of the room was busy with their own cases. Phones rang. A random mix of voices traveled our way. The mayor didn't care about any of it.

Nix sat at his desk, the chair pushed back so his long legs had lots of room. He was slouched a bit, indicating that while he'd give Nash respect, he wasn't cowed by the guy.

I leaned a hip against Nix's desk, and our boss, the chief, rested his shoulder against the entry to his office, which was a few feet away. I'd left the party before Nix, but he didn't look too rough. I'd never known him to drink hard and assumed he was more inclined to be sober so he and Donovan could take Kit home for a little fun. If he was tired, it would be from that.

As for me, the few hot rum drinks had worn off courtesy of Shane and Finch. I hadn't driven home—I wasn't that stupid—but had crashed in Poppy's guest room. I wasn't hungover, but I wasn't eager to be here either. My bad mood wasn't from the mayor, but from the fact that I'd let two hot cowboys get in my pants. And my head.

I'd tossed and turned thinking about Shane and Finch, about how they'd touched me. How they'd made me come. They'd done everything they said they would, although they'd pushed it at the end. They wanted more. I didn't. So I walked.

While I listened to the mayor, I wondered if I'd made a terrible mistake.

"You're well aware Dennis Seaborn took up a week of our time," Nix said.

I turned my thoughts back to the case. The man had turned himself in, confessing to the crime, but it turned out he hadn't done it.

"As for Erin's parents, they might want answers, but they're the ones who messed with the case," Nix reminded the mayor. "If they hadn't paid off Seaborn, we wouldn't have lost all that time."

The mayor's jaw clenched.

"They're not being charged with obstruction of justice only because you told us not to," the chief reminded him.

Our boss, fortunately, wasn't into politics. He was close to retirement age but hadn't checked out yet. He was all for finding out the truth, not kowtowing to the

Cutthroat elite. The Mills were in that camp, and they were the ones who'd paid Dennis Seaborn a lot of cash to admit to the murder of their daughter. We assumed it was because of their son, Lucas, and his thin alibi.

I wasn't close with my family—hell, my father had run off when I was five, and I hadn't talked to my mother in years. Lucas Mills, though, had to deal with parents who thought he'd killed his own sister and paid a dying man to take the fall. I wasn't going to share my opinions on them with the mayor. The chief had said it perfectly.

"They're grieving," the mayor replied. "Out of their minds."

They were out of their minds, all right, but not with grief. Nix and I had met with them many times since the murder. They'd emptied Erin's house within days of her death, and it was up for sale as if she'd never existed.

"The fingerprints are all back from Erin Mills's house. Everyone's either been ruled out or cleared. There was no sign of a break-in. She knew the person or let them in voluntarily. The only thing disturbed was the trophy used to bash her head in."

The mayor tapped his chin with a finger. "What about the roommate?"

"Kit Lancaster?" I asked.

He nodded.

"She was cleared."

Nash knew all this. His son, Donovan, was dating Kit. Either father and son didn't get along or Nash didn't like Kit. Who brought up his son's girlfriend as a possible murder suspect if he liked her?

He knew the deal. Knew exactly where we stood in the investigation. Every time he asked, the answers were the same.

"Give me something new," he said.

Nix leaned forward, set his elbows on his thighs. "There is nothing new."

"So the case is going to go cold? What am I going to tell the town?"

"It is an ongoing investigation," I said, giving him the political statement he wanted.

The mayor sighed, slowly shook his head, then walked away.

The chief didn't say anything until the guy was out of the room. "He's a decent mayor, but he's a total asshole."

I stifled a smile. Nix laughed outright.

"Go home," the chief said, pushing off the doorframe. He grabbed his coat from the coatrack in the corner beside the philodendron. "Unless something new comes in over the weekend, I'll see you Monday morning."

He walked off, and I glanced at Nix. We'd been so focused on this case that we'd been doing overtime for weeks. The party the night before was the first time I'd seen Nix in a social setting since the murder. The chief knew we'd followed all the leads we'd had. He knew a case could sit cold for some time before there was a break. We were in that lull now. He knew it. Nix knew it. I knew it. The mayor didn't believe in lulls, clearly. But there was no thread to follow, at least today. Neither of us needed to be told twice. We left the building and the Mills case behind.

$\mathcal{E}$VE

As soon as I got in my car, I called Poppy to let her know my weekend was free.

"We can veg and watch movies," she said, her voice high-pitched like a fifteen-year-old girl.

She immediately invited me to stay since the weather was supposed to be bad. Snow was already falling and covered the streets, making Cutthroat look like a picture postcard. I would usually ski with the new powder on the slopes, but I felt like being lazy. Snacks, sweats and movies with a friend sounded perfect.

I lived downtown in a little house built for a miner's family back in the late 1800s. It was tiny, only a living room, kitchen, bedroom and bathroom—which had been added on as a little bump out since when it was originally built, there had only been an outhouse.

I loved the wood floors, the big windows. The cute fireplace. But if we were doing a girls' weekend, my place was too small. My couch wasn't big enough for someone to sleep comfortably, and I wasn't sharing a bed with Poppy.

"I'm taking a nap," I added, eager to indulge in that daytime treat.

"I can't believe the mayor let you take a day off," she said once I was well out of town. Her voice came through the dashboard speakers since my cell was synced with the car.

"He didn't." I told her about the meeting, how Nash had left in a huff.

"I want this case closed as much as you, but you deserve a break. I'm not trying to be mean or anything, but Erin's not coming back. She'd want you to watch movies with me."

That made me smile. "She would, huh?"

Poppy had known Erin Mills. They hadn't been friends since Erin had been a few years younger, but they'd traveled in similar circles. The rich circles.

I took a turn onto one of the county roads that led to Poppy's place. The wheels turned, but the car kept going straight, sliding on ice hidden beneath the fresh snow. I swore under my breath. I wasn't going fast, but there was no chance of stopping. I knew the drill. I didn't press the brakes and turned away from the turn. That helped a little, but I still slid off the road.

"Shit," I muttered.

"What's the matter?" she asked.

"I just slid off the road," I said, relaxing my fingers around the steering wheel. I took a deep breath, let it out.

"Are you hurt?"

"No, I'm fine. But I slid about five feet into a ditch."

I gently set my foot on the accelerator, turned the steering wheel up toward the road. The wheels spun, and I immediately stopped. Putting the car in reverse, I tried again, the other direction. The car moved two feet, but then the wheels began to spin again.

"Yeah, I'm stuck. I'll need to be pulled out."

"I don't have a tow rope, and I don't think my SUV is powerful enough to pull you out."

I sighed. I could walk, but it was a few miles still to Poppy's house. I was nowhere near town, and the backroads were not frequently traveled. My boots, coat and hat would be fine against the cold, but for only so long. Besides, since I'd slid off the road, someone else could easily slide and hit me if I were walking.

"I'll call a tow truck," I said, knowing I was safer staying in the car.

"I'll call Shane," Poppy offered at the exact same time.

My heart rate kicked up again, this time from the name alone, not a treacherous slide on ice.

"You don't have to do that," I said instantly. "I'm sure someone will drive by and be able to help." Why had I ever thought I could have a fling with them? They'd offered, but I'd accepted. I'd consented to getting a *sample*. And wow, had they given me a sample.

I wanted more. If the orgasm they'd given me had been from oral sex, I could only imagine a dick-induced orgasm might make me pass out. And there were *two* of them. Two dicks would probably kill me. But what a way to go.

I'd fooled around, then fled. Yeah, I'd been the one to set the parameters. No relationship. No emotions. Just sex.

I couldn't do it though. It had been *too* good. There was something about Shane and Finch, and not their sexual skills, that attracted me to them. I wanted more, and not just sex. I wanted to get to know them.

And that couldn't happen. Men were assholes. They fled when things got tough. They were mean. They hit. They wanted absolute control. I wouldn't go back to the woman I was, weak and defenseless. Chad had blamed everything on me. Dinner not being done. A lost sock. The battery dead in the car. Hell, even bad weather. He was a manipulator, an expert in passive aggressiveness. I could never do anything right, and I'd believed him. He'd slowly isolated me from my friends. I'd been in a bad place, a place I swore I'd never be in again.

I couldn't, *wouldn't* go back there.

The threat was real and twice as bad because I was interested in Shane *and* Finch.

"You're not waiting for someone to drive by. And I'm sure a tow's going to take a while. I'm calling Shane... unless there's a reason why I shouldn't?" she asked.

I rolled my eyes, wishing she could see me. "I don't know what you're talking about."

"Uh-huh. You left in a rush, and it was because of a guy. I know it."

"I'm in a ditch, Poppy, miles from town. It's snowing. I'm not getting into it now."

"So there is something between you." She laughed.

"Poppy," I groaned.

"Why not talk now?" she countered. "It's not like you're going anywhere."

Internally I fumed. She was right. I couldn't be the only person who'd slid off the road in this weather. Hardin and Mac had one tow truck, and I had no doubt they were busy today. People in Cutthroat were super nice and stopped if someone needed help. But being in law enforcement made me wary of strangers stopping, especially with a murderer on the loose. I had an option to get out of this predicament, and I was being stupid not to take it.

"Fine, call Shane."

She hung up without saying goodbye. Not two minutes later, she called back. "They're on their way."

My heart did that funny leaping thing again. *They* were on their way.

"Your party was great," I told her, trying to steer the convo to something safer than Shane and Finch. "I've never been to a bonfire in the winter before."

"It's winter forever around here," she said. "Might as well make the most of it."

I'd grown up in Colorado and was familiar with winter and snow. But Montana was colder, darker and was buried in the white stuff for months. Besides that, there was no spring, only snow until one day it became summer, sometime in June.

"You left in a rush," she stated. "It *was* because of Shane. Right?"

She could be a detective with how perceptive she was.

"I was tired." I'd been far from it. I'd gone to her guest room, gotten in bed and relived every second of the time with Finch and Shane. How Shane had a dimple in his left cheek when he smiled. How Finch's whiskers had felt on my inner thighs. The way Shane had kissed. How Finch had known just how to play with my nipples to make me wet. How Finch's tongue could be magic on my clit. And his finger... I hadn't even known I had a G-spot.

I'd tossed and turned thinking about how stupid I'd been to walk away from two gorgeous guys while at the same time believing it had been smart to push them away. If they got too close, they'd see the cracks, know I was broken in so many ways. One guy had destroyed me. I wasn't letting two get near my heart.

She sighed. "I'll get the truth out of you eventually, especially if you're staying here all weekend."

In the rearview mirror I caught a glimpse of a truck headed toward me, and I followed it as it slowed, then stopped.

"Someone's pulled over to help. I've got to go."

"Fine, you can use that excuse. I want details later."

"Poppy, I'm not sharing things about your brother."

"Ha! I knew it was him."

"Enough!" I couldn't help but laugh. "Really, I've got to go."

The pickup truck was a newer model, huge, had double wheels in the back and was towing a trailer with two snowmobiles on it.

The doors opened on the truck, and two men stepped out at the same time. They turned to face me, and my mouth went dry. My heart skipped a beat, and my breath caught. Oh fuck, I'd forgotten how gorgeous they were.

Finch and Shane walked my way. Their long-legged gaits ate up the distance. Both wore jeans and sturdy leather boots. Finch had on his cowboy hat, and the collar on his jacket was lifted around his neck. Shane wore a black down coat and a gray watch cap tucked over his ears.

My body heated, remembering what we'd done, how they'd made me feel. The chemistry had been off the charts. And now, ogling them, I still wanted them. Wanted more, wanted that bed Finch had mentioned. And them in it.

There was no avoiding them now, especially when they came down the ditch's incline and approached the driver's door.

I pushed the button, and my window slid down. Cold air rushed in, along with their scent of soap and man.

Shane stepped close. "Are you okay?"

I nodded. "I'm fine. Just slid right off. You were here really quickly. Poppy just called you."

"We were going snowmobiling and weren't too far from here. You sure you're not hurt?" I met Shane's dark eyes, refused to look away. I felt it, that kick, the chemistry. It was as if he could see past all the defenses I'd put in place. Past everything to see *me*.

It was that look that had gotten them into my panties last night, that had me wanting them back in them again.

No! I shouldn't. But like a decadent box of chocolates, one wasn't enough. I wanted more with both of them.

"Think you can pull me out?"

"She's not going anywhere," Finch called, coming around the hood. Snow covered their shoulders and their hats. "At least the car. Looks like the front axle's bent."

I closed my eyes for a second, took a deep breath of the freezing air. "I was headed to Poppy's. Think you can drop me there? I'll call Mac to pick the car up when it's convenient for him."

"No," Shane said.

I frowned. "No?"

Finch slowly shook his head.

"No?" I repeated.

"You're not going to Poppy's. You're coming home with us."

"What? Why?"

"We have unfinished business from last night. You got your sample," Finch said, his breath coming out in white puffs of steam. "Now you get the real thing."

Shane looked up at the sky, big fat snowflakes falling on his face. "This storm's not stopping anytime soon. A perfect time to stay in bed. With us. When do you have to be back to work?"

I was a little panicked. What they were offering was what I wanted. Sex, with them. Somehow I'd forgotten how big they were. The intensity of their eyes. The rough corners of their jaws. Their scents. But stuck in a snowstorm with them with no way to leave?

"Oh, um... Monday."

Shane looked to Finch, who nodded. "Perfect."

Perfect?

"You've got a plow on the front of that big truck," I said, my words practically running over each other. "If you don't want to take me to Poppy's, you can get me back to town."

"We could, but won't," Shane said.

I narrowed my eyes. "You're kidnapping a police officer?"

Finch grinned. "When you go back to work on Monday, you can file a report. Tell them we kidnapped you, held you against your will. You be sure to tell them we fucked you so hard that's why you're walking funny. To put as much detail into the report as possible—because I know you detectives are all about the details—you'll list all the places in my house we're going to fuck you and give a tally of the orgasms we wring from you."

I licked my lips. "Poppy's expecting me."

I thought Shane might want to keep his and Finch's kidnapping plans a secret, especially from his sister. It *was* just sex. He only shrugged. "You'll text her on the way and tell her the change of plans."

"I don't want a relationship," I prompted. "She'll think this is a date."

"We offered no strings," Shane reminded me. "As

for Poppy, she might be my sister, but I'm sure she tries not to think about my sex life."

I rolled my eyes. She might not be interested in his, but she was interested in mine. Although if she didn't want the 411 about where her brother put his dick, she might lay off me.

Still... "You said when you know, you know."

Finch nodded. "That's right. We know, but you don't. We'll get you there."

Shane looked up at the sky once again, and snow fell onto his face, melted instantly. "Fuck, it's freezing."

"You're coming with us, sugar." Finch opened the door, and Shane stepped back to allow me to get out.

"That's right, she will be," Shane said. He winked and a thrill shot through me at the double entendre. "Be sure to grab the handcuffs."

My nipples were hard, my panties ruined. I could pull out my gun and force them to take me to Poppy's. Hell, I could just tell them no. I didn't really want to, and they knew it. I hated that they did, that somehow they knew me so well. That they wanted me to take the choice away. I had consent, but they were making the decision. I'd been the bold one the night before, but all sexual assertiveness had fled when I had. I needed them to tell me they still wanted me, that they were willing to be with me on my terms.

No-strings sex. I wanted it with them. Denying myself was stupid.

"That's right," Finch murmured, his light brown eyes brimming with heat. "It's my turn to use them on you."

"Okay," I whispered. Because really, what else was there to say?

6

SHANE

"You both live here?" Eve asked, looking around.

"I do," Finch said. "If you couldn't tell from this"—
he took his hat off his head, held it up for a second,
then set it on the hook beside the door—"I'm a
cowboy through and through."

We'd left all our outerwear in Finch's large
mudroom and went into the kitchen. Finch was
practically OCD, and there wasn't a thing out of place.
While the scent of coffee lingered, there were no
dishes on the counter, no dirty pans in the sink.

"I work for the Forest Service," I said, leaning

against the counter. "While I have a place in town, I hardly ever stay there."

"Hardly?" Finch said. "Try never."

"I'm stationed at the South Point access, and there's a small cabin for the ranger," I explained. There were multiple access points to the National Forest land. Anyone was welcome to use it for recreation—that's what it was for—but it was my job to ensure people stayed safe, followed the rules and didn't do anything stupid, like try to leave food out for a bear.

Eve cocked her head to the side. "Wow, that's... um, great."

"Didn't peg me for a ranger?"

She shrugged her slim shoulders. She wore black jeans, a pale blue sweater that was damned soft to the touch, and thick socks.

"Based on the snowmobiles you two were pulling, you like the outdoors, no matter what the weather."

"True enough. I don't like crowds." I scratched the back of my neck. "Hell, I don't like people all that much."

"You kidnapped me," she reminded me.

I walked over to her, took her hand and gave it a little squeeze. "That's because I like *you*."

"Thirsty? Hungry?" Finch asked, standing beside the fridge. Eve turned his way.

She shook her head. "No, thanks. What does your ranch do? Alfalfa? Horses? Winter wheat?"

"Cattle," Finch replied. "Beef. Anderson Farms has been around for generations."

"You live here alone?"

"My parents divorced when I was young. Mom couldn't handle the winters. My dad has dementia and lives in a memory care place in town. It's just me here now."

"He must be a great guy."

I remembered Mr. Anderson before the disease took over. He was quiet, kind and hardworking, just like Finch.

Finch nodded but said nothing.

She tipped her head to the side and studied him. "I get my beef under plastic in the supermarket, not with four hooves and a moo."

I shook my head, hooked my arm around her waist and led her to the family room. "Finch has a thousand acres and specializes in free range. He doesn't sell to the conglomerates who transport to feed lots in Colorado."

"I know about them. I grew up there."

"In Colorado?"

She nodded. "Small town an hour up in the mountains from Denver."

Finch followed and went to look out the big window. His land was obscured by the heavy snow. "I'm not interested in talking about my beef. Not unless it's this."

He pointed to the thick bulge in his jeans. He cupped his dick, gave it a squeeze.

"Oh my God," Eve said, then started to laugh. "Seriously?"

He shrugged, but his mouth was turned up in a sly smile. "No strings. That's what you wanted. That means no small talk. Let's fuck."

"Just like that?" she asked. Her eyes were wide, clearly stunned by Finch's boldness. She wasn't a fuck-and-forget type. We'd known that right away about her, and it pissed me off the way Finch was talking to her.

He wasn't that kind of guy. But he was playing the part she wanted. For now. She might be able to ride our dicks for the weekend and think herself completely free and clear of any kind of emotional detachment. It wasn't her. She got involved, invested in people's lives. That was who she was—it was obvious even in the short amount of time we'd known her— and why we wanted her so much.

Not everyone would defend a friend's house from burglars in their underwear.

She wasn't a virgin, but I doubted she'd ever picked up a guy at a bar before. It wasn't in her nature to be shallow. Her job dug into people's lives and wanted to know them. By the look on her face, she wanted to know more of us, wanted more than just a quick fuck, but was almost desperate to keep us at an emotional distance.

This was good news. We had a chance. A *real* chance.

I turned her to face me, set my hands just above her ass, my fingers sliding into the back pockets of her jeans.

"You call the shots, Eve." She tipped her chin up to look at me. Fuck, she was pretty. I hadn't noticed the spray of freckles across her pert nose in the dark the night before. They were faint, but her skin was pale so they stood out. Her cheeks were flushed, her lips full. There was a tiny indent in her chin. It was her eyes though, big for her face, that held so much. Wariness, eagerness and more. She'd seen a lot in her job, I was sure. And yet she was here, with two almost-strangers. That showed she trusted us, even if it was only subconsciously.

Being Poppy's brother certainly helped.

"You did last night. You do now. Sure, we kidnapped your ass, but you came with us all on your own," I added.

"Yeah, you could have tasered us if you didn't want to come," Finch said. "A no would have worked, too."

She pursed her lips and gave a funny eye roll, knowing we'd called her out. She said nothing, so I pushed on.

"You want more of what we gave you last night?" I asked. My dick was hard, and I wanted to reach down and adjust it. The only way it was going to be more comfortable was if I opened my pants and let it out, and I wasn't doing it until she said yes.

Eve held my gaze, then looked to Finch. Then back. She nodded.

"We need the words," I prompted.

She swallowed, licked her lips. "Yes. I want more like last—"

Before she could finish the sentence, I bent at the waist and tossed her over my shoulder to carry her to Finch's bedroom.

"Cuffs in your bag, sugar?" Finch asked.

"Oh my God, you two are obsessed with those handcuffs," she grumbled from upside down, then laughed.

"While we won't use them this first time, they're definitely coming out to play," I promised.

————

EVE

SHANE DROPPED me onto the bed. They stood side by side at the foot of it, staring down at me. I felt like prey that had been cornered, ready to be devoured. I'd been wet ever since they climbed from their truck on the side of the road. It seemed I had a thing for cowboys. Who knew?

"You're wearing too many clothes," Finch said.

I had to agree with him because it was too warm in here. Finch's bedroom screamed male. A huge bed for a huge man. Tan walls, lots of stained wood—floor, trim, furniture. A big window looked out over his ranch. A glass door was to the right of it, and while all I could see was snow, I assumed there was a patio buried beneath.

Shane tipped up his chin. "What color panties and bra do you think she's wearing today?"

I looked back at the two of them. Jeans, flannel shirts, brawn that went on for miles. I'd only known them when they were together, so their combined scent was slightly woodsy but all male. Finch's chocolate gaze raked over me. "Black."

Shane licked his lips. "Let's find out." Leaning down, he grabbed an ankle and slid off one wool sock.

Finch took off the other.

I lay there and watched. I could take off my own socks. I could certainly undo the button on my jeans and slide down the zipper. The only help I offered was lifting my hips.

"I hope you got those panties on sale," Finch said, his voice deep and grumbly.

I lifted my head and looked down my body. "Why?"

"Because it's barely more than a scrap of satin."

I bit my lip and tried not to smile. He sounded angry at the sight of my thong, but when I saw the thick outline of his dick through his jeans, I knew he was far from it. I was so thankful I'd shaved in the shower earlier. While I hadn't thought I'd see Finch and Shane again, I was damned glad I'd put on my prettiest underthings this morning. By the looks on their faces, I'd be sure to wear only the raciest scraps of lingerie from now on.

Wait. That meant I wanted to please them. That meant I wanted more than just today.

Finch set a knee on his bed and tucked his big fingers into the ribbons that made the sides of my thong and slid them off. Just the feel of his knuckles brushing over my bare skin made me shiver.

He held up the panties, looking so small dangling from one finger, then tucked them into his shirt pocket. "Purple. My new favorite color."

I was bare from the waist down. I didn't have time to feel awkward because Shane dropped to his knees, grabbed my ankles and pulled me to the edge of the bed, setting my legs over his shoulders.

I gasped and pushed up onto my elbows. "Shane!"

He was eyeing my pussy—which was *right there* in front of his face. He took a deep breath. "Yes?"

"What are you—"

"If you don't know, then Finch wasn't doing it right."

"As if," Finch grumbled. "She dripped all over my face when she came."

I could feel my cheeks go hot, along with the rest of me, remembering what he'd done.

"You're dripping wet now." Shane slid a finger up and down my slit, parting me. "So pretty." I gasped again but watched as he held the finger up, then licked the moisture from it. "You're right. She is sweet."

I stared at him, couldn't believe how hot it was. His

dark hair, stubbled jaw, heated gaze... all between my thighs.

"You going to watch me eat your pussy?" he asked.

I couldn't help but nod. "I'll say yes to anything right now."

He grinned, licked his lips, then lowered his head.

"Oh my God," I moaned, watching his tongue flick the path his finger had taken. He continued to lick me as he lifted his gaze, watched me.

I couldn't hold myself up any longer and flopped back onto the soft mattress. Shane chuckled just before he went to town. His mouth settled over my pussy and did ridiculously magical things. Tongue flicking and swirling. Sucking. Nibbling. Then his fingers got involved.

"Let's get the rest of your clothes off, sugar." Finch's voice was low, and I felt the bed shift as he moved beside me.

Shane grabbed hold of my hips, held me tight so I wouldn't move as Finch helped me lift my torso enough to strip me of my sweater and tank top. Even my bra. "Fuck, you're so damned pretty," he murmured when I lay on his bed once again, now completely bare.

I didn't open my eyes. I couldn't. What Shane was doing was incredible. I was close to coming, which was rare for me. Until last night and Finch. In the past I'd had a guy go down on me, but it had never felt like this and I'd never come. As for Chad, he'd refused to do oral.

I grabbed Shane's head, tangled my fingers in his hair. Pulled him closer, tugged him up, moved him where I wanted him. My thighs clenched around his ears and I was sure I was smothering him, but I didn't care. I was going to come.

And then I felt the hot, wet suction of Finch's mouth on my nipple. It was such a shock, a surprise that I clenched, then came on a scream.

In the moment I was surprised women liked to fuck just one guy. Two... holy shit, who knew? And we hadn't actually had sex yet.

Shane didn't stop. His tongue still circled my clit in some sort of imaginary alphabet he knew and my pussy loved. His finger continued to curl and rub over my G-spot. Finch switched to laving my other nipple, his hand cupping my breast. They didn't let up at all. Shane, though, added a second finger to the mix, pressing the slick tip to my back entrance. It was a gentle brushing over the sensitive tissues, and I bucked off the bed.

I felt the vibrations of a small laugh against my pussy. "Never played with your ass, have you?"

I shook my head, my hands now falling to Finch's shoulder and head. He felt bigger and different than Shane, reminding me that they were both here with me.

They might be two men who wanted me, but they were two *different* men. Unique in their own way. Yet both of them were attracted to me. Were eager to satisfy me. Whose dicks, stuck in their jeans, were hard for me.

"I like it. Don't stop," I ordered.

"Yes, ma'am," Shane said, continuing his play.

I'd just had one orgasm, and a second quickly followed. I had no idea my ass had nerves or something that made me so hot I felt myself getting wetter. A slight bit of pressure of his finger on my virgin ass and I came. There was too much going on. My mind couldn't keep up. I let go. Gave over. Sank. Fell. Submerged. Reveled.

I bucked and writhed, called out their names and swore like a sailor. I tugged on Finch's hair, dug my nails into hard muscle. I felt my pussy gush with arousal, ready for a cock next. My nipples were painfully hard, and Finch had been gentle with them.

My mouth was dry, my breathing ragged.

"I'm not going to make it," I said finally.

Shane was kissing my inner thigh, Finch stroking

his hand over my body as if he couldn't stop touching me. "Oh?"

"You haven't even gotten your dicks in me yet. I think they might kill me."

I blinked my eyes open, looked up at Finch. Shane crawled up my body, my thighs still spread wide. They were gorgeous, generous and fun. And they were all mine. At least for right now.

Finch moved to stand beside the bed, took off his clothes. I lay there, replete and sated, and watched. He gripped his dick, huge and thick in his tight hold, and began to stroke it.

"Just think, sugar. What a way to go."

7

 INCH

Fᴜᴄᴋ, she was incredible. Feeling her come on my mouth the night before was so much different than watching now. Sure, it was a little weird to *watch* two people going at it, but it was Shane and Eve. It didn't turn me off, only made my dick even harder.

The ability to observe, to see the way Eve's skin flushed a pretty pink, the way her nipples hardened after I'd removed her heavy layers of clothes. The way her mouth opened on a gasp. The sight of her legs thrown over Shane's back.

She was passionate and held nothing back. Not

from me the night before—and we'd been behind a barn where we could have been discovered—or now, sprawled out on my bed.

Maybe that was why I was so content. She was in *my* bed. I'd never had a woman here before. I'd never snuck a girl in when I was a teenager, not with my dad's room right down the hall. Once I had the house to myself, I still kept this place off-limits. My sanctuary of sorts. Sure, I fucked. But either at the woman's place or a locked bathroom at a bar or even the supply closet at the seed and feed.

I'd never wanted a woman here. Until now.

She looked right, her dark hair a wild tangle across my blanket. Her hands gripping the down as if she might fly away. Later I'd be able to breathe in her scent, know she was mine.

She was. She just didn't know it yet.

"Are you just going to stroke that thing or put it in me?"

I blinked, realized I'd been staring at her, feeling so fucking pleased with myself that I was going to fuck her that I got distracted from actually fucking her.

I didn't say anything, just went to the nightstand and grabbed an unopened box of condoms. I pulled out a strip, tore one off and dropped the rest on the bed.

"Not getting in you until I keep you safe," I said, rolling the condom down my length.

Shane stood, wiped his mouth with the back of his hand.

"Decide how you want to be fucked, sugar. I can grab your ankles and sit them on my shoulders and slow fuck you to come again. Or you can flip over and I can pound you from behind nice and deep."

"How about both?" she asked.

I couldn't help but grin. "Fuck, yeah."

Moving to stand between her parted knees, I did just as I said and took hold of her ankles and set them on my shoulders. I was too tall to get right in her, so I leaned forward, setting a hand on the bed by her hip. Her knees bent and were up by her tits.

I took a second to ensure bending her this way worked for her. She didn't wince or pull her legs down, only lifted her hips so her pussy bumped against the head of my dick.

Gripping the base, I lined up and pressed into her in one long, slow stroke. I watched as her pussy lips parted around me, how she stretched open to take my width and her inner walls milked and clenched, adjusting to how deep I could go.

"Sugar," I growled.

"Why aren't you moving?" she asked on a breathy

pant as she tried to roll her hips. It took me deeper and I groaned. Sweat beaded on my brow, and my balls drew up with the need to come.

Fuck, she felt so good. Hot, wet, tight. So incredible.

"Bossy little thing, aren't you?" I pulled back so just the head was opening her up, then plunged deep.

"Yes," she cried.

That was the one word I wanted to hear. I took her hard, fast. I was too far gone, her pussy too perfect. Her breasts were small, but they bounced each time I slapped my hips against her ass.

I was going to come, but not until I pleased her. Eve came first. I pulled out with a hiss, grabbed hold of her ankles and rolled her onto her stomach.

"Crawl up, sugar. Show me that ass."

She looked over her shoulder at me. Gorgeous. Her hair was mussed, her cheeks flushed. Her lips were parted, and her breasts bounced with her ragged breaths.

"Hang on, I want in on this."

I hadn't paid Shane any attention, but he was naked now, his dick hard and curved up to bump his belly. It was already covered with a condom. He dropped onto the bed, head on the pillows. He curled a finger, and Eve crawled up and over him.

She dropped her head and kissed him, all the while showing off her ass, her knees spread wide around Shane's hips. Pink pussy lips were all but dripping with her desire. They were swollen from fucking and open. I watched as both her holes winked at me as she clenched.

I couldn't wait a second longer to get back inside her.

I moved up the bed, knelt behind her. Shane bent his knees and spread his legs wide to give me room.

Sliding right back in was easy, and I groaned at the feel. I set my hands on her hips. While she was lean and muscular, she was soft and cushiony beneath my palms. Her moan was stifled by Shane's mouth.

I worked her at a slow pace, not wanting to stop Shane from enjoying her too. That didn't keep me from trying out her ass like Shane had. I licked my thumb, then set it over her tight little back entrance. I didn't push in—I wasn't fucking stupid—only circled gently.

Her head came up, her hair tossed down her back. "I... I love that."

I couldn't help but smile. "We'll get you ready, sugar, for us to take you there. Not today, but soon."

"Give me a turn at her pussy," Shane said.

I paused, thought about what he wanted, then caught on.

Slowly I pulled out. "Give Shane a turn," I told her.

Eve looked over her shoulder at me, then back at Shane. She shifted so she hovered over his dick, then lowered down. From behind, I got to watch my friend's dick disappear inside her.

His hands moved to her hips as he helped her ride him.

"My turn," I said after a little while.

Eve laughed as she lifted off Shane and stuck her ass out for me. I didn't wait, just plunged back in.

"You've got two dicks to take, Eve," Shane said. "Who's going to get you off? Finch from behind or me?"

I gave it to her good, starting slow and picking up the pace as she pushed back, fucking herself on me. Then she leaned forward, came all the way off, then lowered herself onto Shane.

Back and forth she went until she found a rhythm, her breath picking up, her eyes falling closed as she worked herself on both of us. Her hand moved to her clit, her fingers rubbing circles over it as she fucked us both.

I didn't give a shit if she needed a little extra help to get there. We certainly weren't skimping. I felt her inner walls clamp down just a second before she came, her head thrown back as she tensed. Cried out.

"Fuck, that's hot," Shane said as he watched her come.

I followed right after her. It was impossible to hold off a second longer, not the way she was squeezing me. I gripped her hips hard as I held myself deep, filled the condom.

I pulled out, let Shane take over as he brought her down on top of him, even while she was still coming, worked her through that orgasm and gave her another. Only then did he follow and bust his own nut inside her.

The condoms were a necessity. We hadn't talked about her being on any kind of birth control, nor did we mention if we were clean. I wasn't interested in being a dad anytime soon, and I respected Eve, and myself, enough to use protection until we worked it out.

But the idea of coming in her without the latex barrier made my dick start to stir. I wanted to mark her, to make her mine. Body *and* soul.

We were doing a damned good job with her body. We just had to get through to her soul next.

———

EVE

I WAS AT MY DESK, staring out the window at all the fresh snow, probably two feet. It had finally stopped overnight, the clouds moving east. The sun was out, and it was almost blinding to look at. Since my car was sitting in Mac's shop—he'd picked it up from the side of the road a few hours after I'd called it in—Finch had dropped me off at the station before taking Shane to his post with the forest service. Fortunately I'd be able to use a department SUV until my car was fixed and wouldn't be reliant on Finch. That was the last thing I wanted, to have to rely on either of them. I was struggling with the no-strings thing, and that would have only made it worse.

Shane had a weapon of his own. Sure, a gun at his hip, but also a uniform. The cliché was true. A guy in uniform was a sight to behold, ruthless for a woman's panties. I should have guessed it, but I'd been too busy enjoying him naked to think about his work clothes.

"Hey," Nix said, walking by to hang up his coat. The room was half full, some people wrapping up their night shift, others coming in to start their day. Phones rang and the scent of coffee came from the break room.

I blinked, realized I'd been spacing out, and glanced his way. "Hey."

"Good weekend?" He looked relaxed and rested.

Did I have a good weekend? Good wasn't the right word. Incredible. Insane. Intense. It was possible I was walking a little funny. Shane and Finch had worn me out. After we'd had sex in bed the first time, we'd moved to the shower, and we'd done more than wash. Over the next day and a half, we'd had sex all over Finch's house. The couch. The kitchen counter. The bench in the mudroom. Even the hallway wall when the bed had been too far away.

They took me together on the couch. I'd been bent over the arm, and Shane had fucked me from behind while I sucked Finch off. The other times it had only been one of them. Shane in the hallway. Finch in the kitchen, although Shane had come in and watched.

And all those times had been during the day. At night I'd been curled up in Finch's large bed between them. They woke me several times just moving me as they wanted to get back inside me. Each and every time they made me come at least once.

That didn't even count when, just before dawn, Finch had handcuffed me to the headboard, and they'd taken turns having their way with me.

I was exhausted. I wasn't used to having sex with

one guy, let alone two. Hell, I'd had more sex in forty-eight hours than I'd had in the past five years. I had no endurance. If this were to continue, I'd need to exercise or something.

While they'd been careful with the cuffs, I could still feel the sharp bite of the metal when I'd tugged against them. My inner thighs were sensitive from whisker burn as Finch had eaten me out before slowly filling me and making me come. It had been almost lazy, as if he were waking me up with orgasms. After that, Shane had wrapped my legs around his waist and all I could do was cross my ankles and take it since my hands had been restrained over my head. My pussy was sore from two huge dicks.

Every time they touched me, I craved more. Even after all the sex we'd had, it wasn't enough. I wanted more of Shane and Finch... and that scared the crap out of me. How could I want *more* when they'd given me so much? My pussy should be broken, my clit numb.

But no.

"Yeah, good weekend," I replied when I realized Nix was waiting for my answer. "I didn't think about work." I'd practically forgotten my name.

He grinned, then dropped into his chair behind his desk. "Me neither. Saturday we hung out at home, and yesterday we skied. I'm surprised I didn't see you up there."

I had a pass to Cutthroat Mountain and spent a lot of time on the slopes. We'd gone together with a group of friends in the past or run into each other at the lift. Not this weekend.

Nodding, I said, "Yeah, I was tied up."

I bit my lip and pulled out my notes from my drawer, trying to seem casual and hoping he didn't notice my blush.

"Ready to meet with the Oldens?" I asked, wanting to switch the topic off my fling weekend.

"Yeah, I passed them in the lobby," Nix said. "I directed them to the coffee machine and where the interview room is. You can meet them in there."

The Mills murder wasn't the only case we had. The Oldens' adult son had stolen money from them and emptied their house of valuables to sell for drugs. While they were devastated by the effects of drugs on their only child, they wanted to press charges, knowing it was best if he faced the consequences for his actions. Donovan Nash was joining us, and we hoped to come to an agreement where the son wouldn't do jail time but be forced into rehab. It was a bad situation, but I had to hope the intervention would put the guy back on track.

"Sounds good." I grabbed my case file and a pen. "Thanks."

An hour later I dropped into my chair, wished my coffee cup was full. The phone on my desk rang.

"Miranski," I said.

"I can't believe you ditched me on Saturday for my brother."

I huffed out a laugh at the way Poppy got right to the point.

"You sent him. Sorry," I replied finally, leaning back.

Nix walked past, empty coffee mug in hand. I reached forward, grabbed my empty cup and waved it at him. He grabbed it and took it with him toward the break room.

"No, you're not."

"You're right. I'm not sorry at all." I tried not to grin, but it was impossible. I wasn't. Two hot men paying complete and total attention to me and giving me countless orgasms? Sorry, not sorry.

"I should hate you, but I'm just glad you two hit it off."

"Three," I said, then bit my lip.

"Three?"

"Us three." I squeezed my eyes shut as I admitted

the truth. Not that she could see me. "Me, Shane *and* Finch."

Poppy was dead silent for a few seconds; then she squealed. "I knew it! You guys are perfect for each other."

I pulled the phone away from my ear so I didn't go deaf as she chattered on and on about how she'd figured they were looking for a woman together. She cited Nix and Donovan, Cy Seaborn and Lucas Mills and even Mac and Hardin as examples of great guys who went their own way when it came to love.

"Perfect? How did you come up with that from the stupid break-in?"

"I didn't. It's just... well, it's obvious now. I should have fixed you guys up a long time ago. You'll make beautiful babies."

I laughed. "Babies? Poppy, this isn't a relationship." I turned my head away from the main room, although no one was looking my way. "It's just sex."

"Okay, I'm going to try not to gag thinking about my brother having sex, but it's not just sex, Eve."

"It is. I made it clear that's all I want."

"Why?"

"Because that's all... I... want," I repeated but said the words slower.

"Again, why?"

"I was hurt by a guy," I said, this time my voice soft because I remembered how weak I'd been, how much it still hurt. "I told you that much. He... he was verbally and physically abusive. I lost myself. I won't do that again."

Poppy sighed. "If anyone can understand, it's me."

She'd never mentioned a bad boyfriend, but I had a feeling the way she and Shane both hated their dad that it was him who'd hurt her.

"I just figured you were waiting for the right one. Or *ones.*"

Shane's grin with that lethal dimple and Finch's whiskey gaze popped into my head. The way they looked when they were deep inside me. When we were sitting on the couch watching a movie. How they touched. Spoke. Everything.

"They won't hurt you," she said. "Not like that."

"They could."

"You wouldn't have gone off with them if you truly believed they'd hit you."

"Poppy, they pretty much kidnapped me."

"And you let them."

I remained silent. I did know they wouldn't physically harm me, but I remembered how I'd felt when I'd walked away from Chad. Empty. Broken. Less. The worst of it all was that I'd been in love with him. That had made it hard to want to leave, but he had destroyed me and I'd known I had to get out.

Looking back, it had been a toxic love and I'd come through the hurt better and stronger. It didn't mean I wanted to go through that again. Heartbreak was heartbreak. It was easier to guard my feelings than to have them destroyed.

"The other night before the party, you had Finch in handcuffs on my floor. Shane was standing there, hands raised in surrender. They could have taken the gun from you, but they didn't even raise a finger."

They hadn't. While Finch hadn't liked having his shoulder torqued, he hadn't resisted. Neither had Shane. Most guys of their size would have, especially with someone smaller like me. They hadn't even touched me. It could have been because I'd been in my underwear, but again, most guys would have done so *because* of that. I hadn't been forward. I'd been barely dressed. I'd touched them first.

"Just. Sex," I said again, perhaps more for myself than for her.

"Fine. When are you going to have *just sex* with them again?"

I could imagine her making air quotes as she spoke.

Nix came back with two steaming cups of coffee

and set one on my desk. I looked up at him and smiled, whispered a thanks.

"You really want the answer to that?" I asked her.

She laughed. "Probably not. They're good guys. Take your time and have fun. Get to know them. You'll like what you discover, I promise."

I'd liked what I'd discovered so far a whole hell of a lot. Their washboard abs. Muscular thighs. Gentle hands. Skilled mouths. Soft words. Powerful thrusts. Deep laughs. Penetrating gazes. Comforting holds. Sexual caresses. "One would think you're getting commission for all the upselling you're doing."

"Shane's had to deal with shit about our dad since... forever and hasn't found a woman that's, well, worthy. As for Finch, you know what happened with him. It hasn't made it easy."

I frowned. "No, what happened with Finch?"

"His arrest." Through the phone I could hear a bell ringing. She was at the middle school a few blocks south of the town library. There weren't snow days in Cutthroat, no matter what the accumulation, so it was Monday as usual for her. "Look, I've got to go to a staff meeting."

She hung up.

Arrest? Finch?

8

 VE

I GRABBED MY COFFEE, took a sip of the dark brew. Nix knew how I liked it with just a splash of milk. Swiveling my chair, I turned to my computer, looked up Finch Anderson in the database. His data came up. It confirmed his address, age and DMV records for his truck, snowmobile. I pushed a few more buttons and ran a criminal history. With high-tech speed, there was his arrest.

Oh shit. Assault.

I glanced up when the chief came in, but didn't pay him any attention beyond a quick hello. How could I when the guy I'd spent the weekend with, the guy who'd handcuffed me to the bed and made me come on his face, had spent three months in jail for assault?

I pushed my chair back, fumbled for my cell in my purse and stood.

"Be right back," I said to Nix but didn't look his way as I walked off. I found an empty interrogation room, shut the door and leaned against it.

I took a deep breath, then dialed Finch.

"Hey, sugar."

"You went to jail for assault and didn't tell me?"

There was a pause.

"That was a long time ago."

"So?" I snapped. I began to pace in the small room.

"Did you read the full report?"

"I got caught on the word 'assault,'" I replied.

"Would you like to hear the full story?" The music that had been in the background cut off. I pictured him in his cowboy hat working in his barn or stable. Fixing his snowmobile. Tossing hay. Maybe he was in his truck.

I sighed, tucked my hair behind my ear. "Yes, of course."

"It was the year after high school. A friend of mine, Shelly Montez, was being harassed by a guy. We'd gone through school together. We weren't close or anything, just hung out some. But there are only so many places to hang out in Cutthroat, especially if you're not old enough to drink."

Whoever used the room last hadn't pushed in the chairs, and I walked around the table and slid them into place absently as I listened.

"That didn't mean we didn't drink, but we couldn't do it in the bars. So we went to people's barns. The back forty of someone's property. Trailheads. Wherever. That time, we were at the Cutthroat lake. A guy was into Shelly, putting the moves on pretty hard. She said no. He didn't like it and grabbed her to go with him. I stepped in and we fought. I won the fight, and Shelly left with her friends. The next day I'm charged with assault. The guy was a Richie Rich from Cutthroat Mountain, and his daddy was pissed."

"You're not exactly the poor kid from the wrong side of the tracks. You have a big chunk of land. I'd say your family has some money."

"That's land, not cold, hard cash. There's no comparison between a trust fund and acreage. I went to jail for three months."

Anger and helplessness settled over me like a heavy blanket. I could only imagine how Finch had felt when he'd done the honorable thing defending a woman and he'd ended up in jail for it.

"Wow." I felt like an idiot for jumping to conclusions. "I'm sorry."

He didn't say anything for a minute, and it made me squirm. "Tell me, sugar. Why are you so upset?"

"Why?" I went to the wall and fiddled with the buttons for the intercom system to the observation room.

"Yeah. All you want with us is sex. It shouldn't matter that I've gone to jail if all you want me for is my dick."

My spine stiffened. "That's not fair."

"No, it's not."

"I have to get back to work." I didn't like this feeling. Remorse, a dash of shame and a whole hell of a lot of confusion.

"You might want just a fling," he began. "It can't be just that for you. You care. Otherwise you wouldn't give a shit about this."

I pursed my lips, squinted my eyes shut, clenched my fist. He was right.

"Sugar, it's okay to care."

I couldn't listen to him any longer. He was getting through to me in a way no one else had in years. I didn't like the helplessness, the sense of vulnerability.

"I've got to go." I hung up, took a deep breath, then another.

Fuck.

I groaned, looked up at the ceiling. I cared for Finch. Shane, too. Too much, obviously, if I felt more than just sexual pleasure with them. I was in such big trouble.

———

FINCH

"You sure she's coming?" Shane asked, checking his watch for the tenth time in five minutes. He paced across his living room as I watched.

I wasn't any calmer, but there wasn't room for both of us to wear out his wood floor, so I sat on the couch, my feet up on the coffee table. As soon as Eve hung up this morning, I'd called Shane. Pissed.

I couldn't believe she'd held the assault against me. Besides the fact I'd done the time, the whole thing had been rigged. It didn't take a rocket scientist to read the report and know that the system had been out to get me. I hadn't gone to Cutthroat Academy. I'd woken up before dawn to do chores with the animals.

I'd never been destined for the Ivy Leagues or to work for a hedge fund so I could buy a ski-in, ski-out mansion on the slope. Shelly's family were farmers, so she and I had been a lot alike. It didn't matter that we helped our families. None of that mattered because Andy Wade had been a pussy and his father hadn't wanted it known he'd had to beat up on a woman to feel good about himself. It had all been tossed onto me.

I'd been too wild. Too angry. Too dumb to know better. So I'd gone to jail. What the record hadn't shown was what had happened since then. Shelly was married now with two kids living on a ranch near Great Falls, happy. Andy Wade had been put into rehab twice before he was twenty-five and was now doing five years for selling cocaine. Daddy hadn't been able to get him out of that one.

"She texted at lunchtime and wanted to meet. Thanks for offering to do it here." I looked around his place. Landscape photos on the walls. Basic furniture. "It's handy that it's just down the street from the station. No way do I want her changing her mind on her drive out to my place."

"No problem. Sometimes I forget I even have it." Shane stopped, glanced about.

I looked around some more. "I think the last time I

stayed here was over the summer when we went to that beer festival."

There was a knock on the door, and Shane rushed to open it. He let Eve in.

"Sorry, I'm a little behind. Mac called and said my car was fixed. I guess it wasn't as bad as it seemed. I went and picked it up." She looked around. "Explain to me how you have this place and you never stay here," she said as Shane took her coat and hat.

"I bought the place after college but quickly learned that when my dad was in town, the paparazzi hounded him and me. I'm sure you've learned popularity by association is a big thing in Cutthroat."

She bent down to undo the laces on her boots, and I almost groaned at the sight of her perfect ass. "Definitely. He was here filming a movie in the fall. I saw him once at the Gallows with a bunch of people."

"That bunch of people were probably all strangers," Shane clarified. "At least to you and me. To him, there are no strangers. I'm not like him. I don't give a shit about popularity. You might want it, but only until you have it. I don't talk with my dad, no matter what the tabloids say about Eddie Nickel, the family man. *Especially* them."

"I take it your dad's not a nice guy?"

Shane's jaw clenched and his eyes narrowed. He

took a deep breath, then spoke. "He hit. Took his anger and frustrations out on me and Poppy. It lasted until I was big enough to hit back. Then he stopped."

"I can see why Poppy hates him," she said, her voice neutral. Flat.

"I wanted to go into forestry, studied it in college. I admit it was partly to spite my dad, but it's what I love. I don't touch a dime of his money. To me, it's all tainted with lies."

"And Poppy burns through it as her own way to fuck with him."

Shane nodded. "The job came with a cabin on government land, and I took to staying there. Simpler. Quiet."

"Can't the paparazzi just follow you out there?"

Shane smiled. "The can and they have. But I'm allowed to carry a gun on forest service land, which gives me an advantage."

She set her boots on the mat by the door and stood back up. "I'll bet." She gave him a small smile, then looked my way. In just her socks, she came over to me. Her hair was long down her back, a little staticky from the dry air.

I stood.

"I'm sorry," she said.

"Sugar, you're not the first person who's been bothered by my time in jail."

"I had access to all the facts, and I still jumped to conclusions."

I appreciated her honesty, the way she owned up to her mistake.

I took her hand, which was fucking freezing from being outside, and pulled her toward the couch. I dropped onto it and tugged her onto my lap.

"This is... I can't remember the last time I sat on someone's lap."

I settled my hands on the curve of her hip and the top of her thigh.

"Get used to it," I all but grumbled. She wasn't getting up anytime soon.

She settled in, shifting, which only made me hard. Fuck, hard-*er*.

She'd apologized. I needed to explain. "I didn't tell you about my record because to me, it didn't matter. It happened ten years ago. I may have been found guilty, but I didn't do anything wrong. Do you want to be judged by some of the things you did years ago?"

She huffed. "Hell, no."

"As I said on the phone, if you're using us just for our dicks, you wouldn't give a shit if I was an ex-con or not. You probably wouldn't remember our names, only that we got you off six ways to Sunday."

"That night at Poppy's party, we said, when you know, you know," Shane said, sitting on the coffee table right in front of us so she was surrounded. "We want you, Eve, and not for just sex. You're more than that. *We're* more than that."

She shook her head. "I can't."

"Can't or won't?" I asked.

Her lips thinned.

"I go with won't," Shane replied, setting his hand on her other thigh. "You feel something for us, and that's what's bothering you."

"You two should be detectives," she replied, her face tipped down so all I could see was her shiny hair.

"Tell us, sugar."

I felt her deep inhale against my chest.

"I moved to Cutthroat to start over. To find myself again." She paused. "Let me back up so it makes more sense. My dad left when I was a kid. Just walked out one day. I barely remember him, only that he had dark hair and a mustache I thought looked like a caterpillar. My mother is bipolar. Now that I'm an adult, I don't blame him for leaving. She's a disaster. I just wish he hadn't left me behind."

VANESSA VALE

"Bipolar's tough." I didn't know much about it, but mental illness in a family member was hard. As a kid?

"When she took her meds, she was good. Not great, but... even. I had meals, clean clothes. She remembered to pick me up from soccer practice. Hell, she remembered I played soccer. When she went off her meds, usually when she felt good for a long stretch because she was *on* them, it was awful. She blamed me for my dad leaving. She yelled, was belligerent. She forgot food. Stuff like that."

I was sure the *stuff* mentioned was a long list. There was probably tons more.

"When I was twenty-two, I met a guy. He was great, until he wasn't. He was like my mom in that he blamed me for things he did wrong. You'd think I would have avoided someone like him *because* of my mom, but maybe that's all I knew. He was late getting home from work so the dinner was cold and he was mad. I wasn't sexy enough and that was why he couldn't get it up. Or, later, why he cheated. I was at the police academy, and he said I was a slut for being around all those men."

"That's all bullshit," I said. The longer she talked, the angrier I became. Not at Eve, but at her mom. At this asshole who needed to be taken care of.

"I know now, but then... I only had my mother,

who should have been a role model, as an example. I thought that what he said was right, that everything I did was wrong. Toward the end, I questioned my ability to do anything. I wasn't sexy. I was stupid. I even started to think I really was a slut for wanting to be a police officer."

"That's ridiculous."

"I know *now*."

"What happened?" Shane asked, his voice just above a whisper.

"He hit me."

Every muscle in my body tensed. "Where is this fucker? I've got acres of land, and Shane's got the entire forest to bury his body."

"I didn't think anything of it. I used makeup to cover it up. Until one day a woman came into the station. Domestic abuse. She told me stories that were really familiar. I'd been trained to offer counseling and a women's shelter, which I did. I remember exactly where I was. It was like a lightbulb went off. I was her. I needed the counseling, that I was being used as a doormat and a punching bag to validate my boyfriend's issues, nothing more."

"Good for you," I said, tipping her chin up with my fingers. I couldn't help but kiss her, to let her know we were here, that we desired her. That she was special.

She moaned, then turned her head away. "If you keep doing that, I won't finish."

I chuckled. She had to feel how hard my dick was at her hip. She couldn't doubt my desire for her.

"I had my partner and a few guys help me move. I never looked back. In fact, I moved here to escape it all."

"What about your mother?"

"She told me I shouldn't have left Chad. That he was good for me, that I was stupid to walk away from someone like him."

I shook my head. "She's a piece of work. I'm sorry, sugar."

She shifted and I let her stand. Sitting, we were both shorter than her. "I left her behind too. Haven't heard from her since I moved here. That's why I freaked with you. I *trusted* myself to spend the weekend with you, and I learned you were arrested for assault. It just made me realize I hadn't gotten any better."

"That's bullshit," Shane said.

"I know. I'm sorry I didn't read the entire case file. If I had, I'd have seen what you did was honorable."

It felt good hearing those words from her. It eased something in me, because it was crucial Eve understand. I wanted nothing between us, especially that shit from my past.

"You don't do relationships because of your ex?" I asked.

She nodded and the hair she'd tucked back fell forward.

"I won't go back to that."

"We're not here to hold you down, sugar," I told her. "We're here to lift you up. You wouldn't want that guy to have this much control over you, would you? Because even after years, he's still messing with you."

She'd been so fucking strong and walked away from an abusive man. A mother who didn't put Eve first... or ever in her life. She was beyond brave. Incredible. Yet avoiding relationships because they'd been shit in the past only meant those who'd hurt her still had control over her.

To break loose, she had to live. To *love.* And that was going to be with me and Shane.

Shane nodded. "We would *never* hurt you."

"I don't doubt you." She set her hand over her heart. "I doubt *me.*"

"At Poppy's party, you went with us around the barn."

She gave a small smile and blushed prettily. "I wasn't thinking with my head."

"Then think with your pussy," Shane said. "It's pretty smart. It wants us, doesn't it?"

She stared at him wide-eyed, then laughed.

"That's what I've been doing wrong all this time? I need to trust my pussy?"

"Abso-fucking-lutely," I told her. "What's it saying right now?"

She bit her lip and glanced at us through her dark lashes. There was her inner sex kitten. She just didn't even know it was there.

"It's saying to have my way with two hot cowboys."

9

 VE

IN LESS THAN FIVE MINUTES, we were naked. I knelt on Shane's bed before them. I was taking turns with them, sucking their cocks, learning every inch of their hard bodies. They stood before the bed side by side. A dick buffet, just for me.

I'd messed up. Epically. Yet Finch forgave me without shaming me, without making me feel like shit —worse than I'd already piled on myself—and moved on. He'd recognized there had been a reason for it. Wanted the explanation instead of backhanding me or walking away.

When I'd told them the truth? When I'd finally opened up about my past, they hadn't used it like a weapon against me, hadn't found me weak for staying as long as I had with Chad. They'd said I was strong.

Strong! Their acceptance of me, their desire to be with me just the way I was, knocked down the last of the walls I'd put up around my heart. I'd been avoiding men in general for so long I'd been blind to how perfect they were. How good. Honorable. Real. Poppy was right. They *were* perfect for me.

I wasn't expecting them to propose marriage, but I was open to more. To see where this took us. And so far it was pretty damned good. I showed them how much by lavishing them with attention. Hands and mouth on their bodies, their dicks.

"Enough," Finch said, setting his hand on my shoulder and moving me back so I sat on my heels on the bed. My mouth popped from his dick like a kid losing a lollipop. "Or this is going to be over before it gets started."

I felt powerful then, knowing I could not only make them feel good, but make them lose control. With the back of my hand, I wiped my mouth.

Shane held up a condom. "We never talked about protection. It's our job to keep you safe. I'm clean and I've never gone without a condom before."

"Same with me," Finch added. "I'd love to go bare with you, but it's your call."

My pussy clenched at the idea of nothing between us.

"I get the shot, so I'm protected from pregnancy. I was tested when I left Chad." I folded my hands in my lap, looked down at how my fingers were clasped together. "I told you I haven't been with anyone since then."

"Sugar," Finch said, his voice so gentle I looked up at him in surprise. "Condom, no condom, your call. What's it going to be? Because we're getting our dicks in you in the next thirty seconds either way."

I couldn't help but laugh at that. "No condom."

Finch sighed and grabbed me, lifted me and dropped me onto the bed. I bounced and he settled over me. "Ready for us?" he asked, his chocolate eyes focused on mine. His hand settled between my thighs and worked my pussy, circling my clit, dipping inside and nudging my G-spot to see. I was wet and quickly writhing beneath him. "You are."

He didn't wait a second longer, just moved his hand away and his cock pushed into me... one inch at a time. The slow friction was incredible. The press of his weight—even though he held himself off me—was comforting.

His pace was slow. Too slow and I told him that.

"I've got a pussy practically strangling my bare dick. I can feel how hot you are. How wet. Nothing between us. I'm taking my fucking time."

I could only nod because I agreed. There was something different about it. Not just the feel but the closeness. I'd shared my dark past with them, my feelings. I was laid bare, not just in body but in heart.

Yes, I was giving it to them. Too fast, definitely, but they were everything I'd imagined and then some. And they had really big dicks and knew how to use them.

Shane dropped onto the bed beside us, began to stroke himself as he watched. "We need to get a plug for your ass. Get it ready for us to claim. Can you imagine? Finch in your pussy like he is now while I'm in your ass?"

I moaned, arched my back at his words. I could imagine it. Between both of them, being taken.

"She likes that idea," Finch growled. "Just got wetter."

"I'm going to come." I was. I did. All from dirty talk and a skilled dick. How had I missed out on man-induced orgasms my whole life?

"Fuck, me too. Too good going bare." Finch thrust deep one last time, filled me. When he pulled back, the hot rush of cum slipped out. I'd never felt that before, his hot release coating me.

He sat back, looked down, saw it. "That's hot as fuck."

Shane shifted up onto his elbow and looked between my legs as Finch moved away. Instinctively I pulled my knees together, but his hand stopped me. "Oh no. Let's see your pussy. All nice and fucked."

I flicked my gaze up to Shane as his finger ran through my folds, feeling Finch's cum and my arousal.

"Your turn," I said, ensuring he didn't feel left out. I had two men, and while big and brawny, they needed equal attention.

He lowered his head and kissed me. And kissed me. And kissed me some more as he slid into me, eased by Finch's cum. He didn't take his time as Finch had, but took me hard, fast with wet, breathy, flesh-slapping-flesh sounds filling the air.

It was perfect. Dirty. Messy. Skin to skin. We came together that time, and all through the night.

———

"DON'T KISS ME," I muttered. "I've got morning breath."

The soft nuzzle of Shane's nose brushed over my

cheek, and his lips settled on my ear, kissing it and working down my neck. He smelled like mint and the soap from the shower.

I was barely awake, content snuggled beneath the heavy blanket. Earlier Finch had stirred me long enough to tell me he had to go. Ranch chores. I had no idea what time it had been, but it had been dark out. Now the soft haze of a winter morning came through the window of Shane's bedroom.

"There are other places I can kiss," he murmured, pulling the blanket and sheet down off my bare body. "If I remember, you liked my mouth on your nipples, the curve of your hip."

I yanked the blanket back up, instantly awake. While the room wasn't cold, it wasn't as warm as under the covers. "Don't you dare!" I gripped the edge of the comforter in a death grip.

"What, you don't like my mouth on your pussy? Last night you screamed about how much you liked it."

I grabbed a pillow and smacked him with it. When I pulled it back, it hit the wall above the bed, and I heard the framed print slide. I glanced up, opening one eye. Seeing that all I did was knock it askew, I shut it again and dropped the pillow beside me.

"I need to up my multivitamin to keep pace with

you two," I grumbled and looked at him. He stood beside the bed, his hair still damp from the shower, and he wore his ranger uniform. He smiled.

"God, you're one of those perky morning people, aren't you?"

"Sure am." He winked.

I groaned, rolled onto my side and rubbed my face against the pillow. "I'm not. My pussy's not awake."

His hand slid beneath the covers, cupped me. "I can wake it up."

I wasn't exactly awake, but I was eager. His hand was magical, knew just how to touch me. Gently, so very carefully at first, as if he knew I might be a little sore. In less than a minute, I was writhing, ready. "I love the feel of our cum in you. Knowing we've kept you well fucked."

God, the words out of his mouth. I pushed the blanket off, and he set a knee on the bed. He undid his belt and opened his uniform pants, pushed them down just enough to pull out his cock.

I lifted my hand to stop him. He frowned down at me. I hadn't rejected him before. I wasn't now, but I needed a moment. "I have to brush my teeth. I can't kill you with morning breath."

He grinned, stroking his cock and eyeing every inch of me at the same time. "Like I care."

"I do," I grumbled. I was aroused, but I was sticking my ground. This thing between us was new, and I wasn't driving him away by my funky breath. I climbed from the bed—the opposite side of where Shane stood—and dashed into the bathroom.

"Hurry, Eve. I don't give a shit about something like that," he called.

I speed brushed, then returned, found him sprawled on the bed, his hands behind his head. Waiting. A man in uniform with his dick out. Holy shit, he was hot.

What a way to wake up.

"You're on top," he said, remaining still and watching me. I wasn't going to argue. The only thing to do in a situation like this was to climb on.

I did. And I took him for a ride, setting my hand on his chest and lifting and lowering, circling. Rubbing my clit all over him. I was wet from all the times they'd fucked me.

He kept his hands where they were behind his head, letting me set the pace, pretty much using him for my own pleasure.

But he came too, right after me, his eyes clenched shut, his muscles tense. I loved the feel of skin on skin, the hot spurts of cum coating my pussy. As it slid down my thighs while I lifted off him and dropped back into bed. I was marked. His.

I closed my eyes, and he got up. I heard the slide of his zipper, the clank of his metal belt buckle. The blanket was tossed back over me.

"Go back to sleep," he said. "You've used me well. Now I've got to head to the office."

"The forest?"

"Yup." I heard his footsteps as he cut through his house, heard the front door close. Then nothing.

The alarm on my cell woke me at eight. I blinked and took a second to remember where I was. It was the third night in a row I hadn't slept at home. The third night in a row I'd been with Shane and Finch. It was a good thing I was alone. I had to get to the station, and I had no doubt they'd get me beneath them—again—and make me late.

Climbing from bed, I pulled myself together. I used the toothbrush from earlier, put on my day-old clothes. I didn't have a new outfit with me, nor makeup or even my hair product, so I had to go home before I headed in.

My cell beeped, indicating a text, and I went over to the bedside table to grab it.

. . .

POPPY: *Do I even want to know what you were doing last night?*

I GRINNED as I texted back.

ME: *Your brother.*

SHE DIDN'T RESPOND. She was probably throwing up. I smiled, grabbed a pillow and tossed it into place, then another. Taking hold of the top sheet, I tugged on it to straighten it. I might not be as neat as Finch, but I liked a made bed. I realized I was smiling. I was last to leave it. The least I could do was make it.

It was when I pulled the comforter up all the way and went around the far side to make it even that I saw it. The black wire that hung down from the bottom of the framed print above the bed. I stared at it, trying to figure out what it was, then knelt on the bed, crawled to the middle to touch it.

I looked around even though I knew I was alone. It was a tiny camera. Over the bed. My heart skipped a beat as I pulled the frame away from the wall just enough to peek behind it. Even in shadow, I could see something was there. I lifted the frame and placed it on the bed beside me. I didn't give a shit about the landscape image, only the wall.

A notch was cut out of the drywall.

"Holy shit."

With shaky fingers, I grabbed the small electronic device. It was the size of a large cell phone, the mini lens plugged into it with a cord about two feet long.

Sitting cross-legged on the bed, I studied the thing. It was a camera of some kind. There was no screen on the unit, only buttons. I spun it around in my fingers, found the catch on the side, opened it. Batteries. I spun it again, found another catch and, when that flap popped open, saw the little memory card.

Getting to my feet, I leaned forward, stuck my fingers into the cutout area, felt around and bumped into something and pulled it free. A small clear plastic case, smaller than a pack of gum. More tiny memory cards.

I looked around the room again.

Shane had a camera over his bed.

Over his fucking bed. Literally. This was the bed he'd fucked me in not even two hours earlier. And the night before with his best friend. Had he taken pictures? Video? Of us? Of me sucking their cocks, of the two of them inside me? Riding them?

I felt sick. Violated. Dirty.

Shane videotaped shit that happened in his bed.

In. His. Bed.

This wasn't a one-time thing because... who the fuck cut a hole in the drywall so the unit would have a place to sit? He had several memory cards along with the camera, which meant he'd done it a lot. He'd taken time to set it all up, so the picture would lay flat against the wall. The camera itself was tiny and could have been missed by anyone—including me—against the black frame.

This was intentional. This was planned and had been in place for a while. He'd said he bought the house after college. This was... oh my God. This was scary as fuck.

I had to see what was on the memory card, but I didn't want to know. Because I had a feeling it wasn't just me I'd discover.

10

I couldn't go to the station. Not with this. Not with what I expected to see. Me. Naked. Getting fucked. No way would I let anyone there see me like that.

I drove to the nearest big-box store, hustled to the electronics section and held up the little plastic case of memory cards. "I need some kind of adapter so I can see what's on here through my laptop."

The guy grabbed something from the case, held it up. It looked like every other random piece of electronic equipment I knew nothing about. "Slip the memory card in here." He pointed to a narrow slit on the side. "Then stick this into the slot in your computer."

I handed him a twenty and told him to keep the change.

Somehow I made it home, although I didn't remember the ride. I tried not to think about Shane, about what I believed he'd done, but it was impossible. I was a detective, knew people had double lives. Husbands who killed their wives and said they'd gone to visit their mothers. Women who intentionally sickened their children to get attention. Hell, even Chad and the verbal and physical abuse. People weren't always what they seemed.

That was why I'd protected myself all these years, from the possibility of getting hurt again. Of being used.

Chad hitting me was nothing compared to Shane filming women without their knowledge during sex. I'd known he'd been with women before, but this?

I dropped my coat on the floor by the front door, went to my desk and pulled the memory card from the camera unit and carefully slipped it into the gadget I'd bought, then put that into the port on the side of my laptop.

A folder opened automatically on the screen, and there were a number of icons to click. The file names were a bunch of numbers and letters, so I double-clicked on one at random.

"Oh my God," I whispered, staring wide-eyed at the screen.

It was a video of a couple having sex, although only the woman was visible since she was on top. She was naked and clearly enjoying herself, lifting and lowering with abandon. Her large breasts bounced and she moaned. I clicked the button in the top corner of the window and closed it. Picked another icon. Another woman on top, the man not visible. God, she was young. Nineteen maybe? Her breasts were large but unenhanced, and they were high and perky. Time and gravity hadn't made them droop at all. Shane was twenty-seven or twenty-eight, too old for teenagers.

The camera had been positioned so it aimed toward the foot of the bed. The angle was too great to see the man on the bottom's upper body, especially his head on a pillow. Shane didn't want to see himself having sex. He only wanted the women he fucked in his pornos.

I closed that one, opened one more.

More of the same.

Three clips. Three videos of Shane having sex with three women without their knowledge. It was well planned because they were all on top. The video was up close. Full frontal. Only a hint of Shane could be seen. The edge of a thigh. Dark thatch of hair at his groin. The shadow of his condom-covered cock when the woman lifted up as she fucked herself.

I ran to the bathroom, bent over the toilet and dry heaved. I hadn't eaten yet this morning, nor had any coffee. There was nothing in my stomach, thankfully.

I knew a guy coming into a relationship would have a past, wouldn't be a virgin. I didn't think any different for Shane or Finch. Based on their sexual abilities, I assumed they had been with many women. We weren't teenagers. Far from it.

But this...

This wasn't notches on a bed. This was illegal. This was unethical. This was... sociopathic.

I wiped my mouth with the back of my hand and went back to my desk. I caught my breath, then clicked more icons. There had to be over fifty different files.

Picking up the little case, I opened it with the edge of my fingernail, shook the contents onto the desk. There were three more mini memory cards. There had to be hundreds of files. Hundreds of women.

I'd been so cautious. So careful and the one and only time I let my heart open, *this* happened.

"Finch," I whispered. I swallowed hard. Tears lodged in my throat. Was he in on it? Did he know?

We'd had sex at his house first. Were there cameras in his bedroom? They'd made it clear from the start they wanted to share me, that together they wanted a relationship with me, but did Finch know about this? Surely, based on the video clips I'd seen, Shane slept with women on his own. It wasn't a two-person thing.

Tears slipped and I brushed them away. How did Shane pull it off? He'd have to turn the camera on, or at least start the recording without the woman knowing. Remote? I opened one icon, then the next, not lingering on the images, just confirming what I saw. Different women all having sex with Shane.

I didn't see myself in any of them. I shook my head. Paused. Took a deep breath. *Focus.* Using the track pad, I changed the folder to list view. The date for each file was there. Nothing from today or yesterday that I could see. The last was a few weeks ago. I clicked that one.

More sex.

I went back further. Opened another.

I gasped, stared wide-eyed at the laptop screen. Erin Mills.

I'd never met the woman, but I'd seen enough images of her to recognize her instantly. Blonde. Early twenties. Really pretty. I could add now that she also had a really nice figure.

She was smiling as she rolled her hips, fucking Shane beneath her. Her breasts were small and pert, the nipples large. I realized her lips were moving. She was talking. I hadn't even thought about the sound. Pressing the button on my keyboard, I upped the volume, cringing as I heard dirty talk. "You love it when I fuck you like this. Your dick is so big. Every time, it's like the first. God, I remember when you popped my cherry." Her voice was soft and breathy.

I licked my lips, tried to remain calm. Analyzed the words. She'd implied it wasn't the first time they had sex and one of the times Shane had taken her virginity. From what we knew of Erin, she'd had sex before her death with Mark Bastion, the ski coach. Kit Lancaster had mentioned a guy named Kurt who'd spent the night with Erin. We'd questioned him, Kurt Vaughn, and he'd confirmed they had a casual relationship. Fuck buddies, he'd said. She'd also slept with Mark Knowles. Three men that we knew of. Plus Shane.

I closed the video, checked the date. Three days before her murder. Fuck.

I had to assume she'd been sexually active for a while, which meant Shane had not only been with her right before she died, but for... years. I took out the memory card, swapped it for one of the others.

Opened it. About twenty files. The dates were all from last year. I took it out, switched it for another. This one had about the same amount of files, but the dates stretched over the previous three years. I checked the last card and found it had the oldest dates. Seven years ago.

I clicked a file. Same bedroom, but the walls in the background were a different color. The foot of the bed was blurry but visible, and the comforter and sheet colors were not the same as the most recent.

This woman was just like the others, on top. She was young. Really young.

Leaning forward, I looked closely at the screen. There on the bed behind her was some clothing. It was a cheerleader top from Cutthroat High School. I recognized it, the blue and gold, the letters *CHS* on the front.

Seven years ago Shane would have been twenty or twenty-one, and he was fucking a high school girl. With the flexibility only someone so young had, she lifted up—without Shane coming out of her—and turned around to face away from the camera into reverse cowgirl. Her dark hair hung long down her back as she picked up her rhythm once again. A man's hand came into view, and it spanked her right ass cheek, then rested there so his thumb could... fuck.

He slipped his thumb into her ass as she kept riding him.

With the sound on, I couldn't miss her squeal of surprise at the spank, then a moan as he worked his thumb all the way into her.

I shut the lid on the laptop. Stared. Remembered how Shane had done the same thing to me the night before. I hadn't been in reverse cowgirl, but straddling and fucking Finch as he finger fucked my ass.

I burst into tears. Let them fall for a few minutes, then pulled myself together.

This wasn't about me right now. It was about the Erin Mills murder investigation. We had no leads—until now. Shane had been with Erin three days before her death. I had to keep digging. I lifted the lid, let the screen come back on. I went through the older files one by one until I found it.

There was Erin Mills again. Standing at the foot of the empty bed. Fully clothed, thank God. This time she was younger. Based on the file date, she was sixteen.

Sixteen.

"You really think I can be in an Eddie Nickel movie?" She looked to the left of the camera as she spoke.

"Definitely. There are sex scenes in movies. It

might be acting, but this isn't something you can fake." The voice was low, and I had to rewind it to hear the words. "Gotta show me your talents."

"I've... I've never done this before."

There was a pause, and the shot dipped and moved as if the camera was picked up.

"You're filming this?" She smiled. "It's a screen test, so of course you are. Okay."

She tugged her top up and over her head, and I turned it off. I couldn't watch it, completely disgusted at what I guessed was going to happen next, especially since she'd been tricked. She'd consented, but she was sixteen, which meant it wasn't consent at all. It was rape.

Shane had made it clear to me how much he hated his dad, so he'd had no intention of helping Erin get into a movie. He'd lied. He'd raped. Took her virginity all for fun. And the cheerleader in the other file? I had to wonder if she'd been eighteen.

I closed the file, switched memory cards to the first one and opened the file from right before Erin's murder. I found the spot where I'd stopped and watched it. Listened.

"When I was sixteen, you said I'd be in an Eddie Nickel movie."

Her smile slipped, and instantly she looked

different. Gone was the aroused, well-fucked look. She stopped moving, looked down at Shane. "You still filming your fucks?"

She looked up at the camera. Dead-on. She knew she was being filmed. Didn't care.

"I wonder if everyone will want to know you like underage girls."

A hand settled on her upper thigh, gripped it, then dropped away.

"Yeah, just what I thought. I'm on set all the time running your events instead of being a star. Get me on-screen or I out you to the media."

All of a sudden, the screen had black shapes, and I realized it was fingers, then it went black. Shane had reached up and turned the camera off.

I stared at the black screen, the file at the end.

I had no doubt I was one of the clips. I had to be, even though I was confident I didn't see any with today's date. I wasn't a tech expert, but it was there. I knew it. Sexual predators didn't change. Never. Even prisoners knew rapists were a class all to themselves. Shane had had opportunity. I'd gone to brush my teeth. He could have turned it on while I was in the bathroom and I'd never know. I'd been on top, just like every other woman.

I was just one in his collection.

This fact made it easier for me to think clearly and objectively.

Shane had a long-standing relationship with Erin Mills. One that lasted years. One where Shane held the power. I was familiar with this concept. Chad had been that way, wielding control over me and making me think I was less. That fucking him and trying to please him would somehow make him love me.

It hadn't. Shane hadn't been interested in any of the women he'd filmed except to get his dick wet. To know he could fuck them and film them without them knowing. That was powerful.

As for Erin Mills, Shane had offered her something he'd never give. Not with how much he hated his dad. He might have even strung her along for years. Perhaps she wasn't confident in her sexuality and instead used sex with lots of men to validate herself. Maybe it was brought about by Shane himself, that very first time. She'd used men to make herself feel better, hoping that someday Shane would come through.

What had made her change her mind this fall? Had she finally had a moment like I had where I realized I'd been wrong, that I'd been used?

In the film clip she'd been powerful. Finally. Had that strength and threat been what pushed Shane to end her? It would ruin him, so he'd killed her to keep her quiet.

But someone like him wouldn't be able to stop. He'd kept his filming a secret for years. He had no expectation of being caught. He knew from me that the case against Erin had gone cold.

"God, he must be laughing his head off, not only fucking the dead woman, murdering her and getting away with it, but fucking the investigator too," I said aloud.

I stood, paced.

Shane needed to go to jail. Now.

I grabbed my cell, called Nix.

"I know who killed Erin."

11

$\mathcal{S}$HANE

MY BALLS SHOULD HAVE BEEN DRAINED, my dick worn out after all the sex we'd had with Eve the past few days. I was hard just thinking about her, and I was standing on the porch of a cabin in the woods. The sun was out, but it was fucking freezing.

Usually I loved the quiet of the woods. No people, no noise. Today it annoyed me. I didn't want to be here. I wanted to be in town, with Eve. I hadn't stayed in my house since last summer, but I was ready to move back there so it would be easy to be with her since the police department was just down the street.

I wanted people. I wanted Eve. And she was twenty miles away in Cutthroat. I couldn't smell her soft scent, only the pine trees. I couldn't taste her pussy on my tongue, only the coffee I'd just finished.

I craved her. After going years with just casual, this... thing we shared was incredible. We'd just gotten her to open up, to see that we would never hurt her, that we'd have her back, that we'd prop her up and stand beside her. All the cliché terms.

I wanted it all with her. I knew Shane did too. Being a rancher, a forest ranger and a detective made for complicated schedules, but we'd make it work. I didn't have to stay here in the cabin. I'd isolated myself from people just as much as Eve had. Remaining here was an easy way to keep people at a distance. We may have gotten past Eve's tough walls, but I realized she'd gotten past mine.

The sound of a car approached, and I stepped off the porch to see who it was. This time of year there were few visitors. Especially now with all the snow. The trail was buried, and snowshoes were needed to get anywhere. Snowmobilers would stick to the service road, but that was two miles south.

It was a police SUV. We did interdepartmental rescues all the time, but no one had called anything in on the radio.

Nix Knight stepped out, and I went to shake his hand. We'd gone to high school together, were friendly, but I wouldn't say friends. I saw him mostly through work these days.

"What brings you all the way out here?"

"I need to bring you in for questioning about the Mills murder."

I frowned, tucked my hands into my coat pockets. "Okay. Want to come in for some coffee first? Just made a pot."

He shook his head. "I'll get you some at the station."

I stilled. "What's going on? You can ask me now, save me a trip in."

Nix sighed. "How well did you know Erin?"

I frowned. "As much as you. Lucas's little sister."

"That's all?"

I huffed. "Are you asking if I fucked her?"

He scratched the back of his neck. "Actually, yes."

"Really?"

He didn't say anything, just watched me. He was using his cop eyes. Something was up.

"No, I never fucked her. I don't think I'd even been by myself with her, let alone got in her pants."

"We have video that proves otherwise."

My eyes widened, and I took a step back. "You have

video of me fucking Erin Mills? It has to be the photographers. They put something together, used some fancy program to put my face or her face on some porn. They hound me. You know that."

"This is definitely homemade."

"Where's Eve? I thought this was her case."

"She's with the videos."

I held up my hand. "Wait. You said videos. There's more than one?"

"Of you and Erin? Yes."

"No way." I turned in a circle, my boots crunching on the snow-packed path.

"Come into town. We have to do this formally."

"You're charging me with *murder*?"

"I'm not charging you with anything. Only asking you questions."

"About a video... videos of me having sex with Erin Mills."

"Yes."

I sighed. "Fine. Let me lock up." I pointed toward the cabin. "I'd like to get to the bottom of this as much as you. I'd rather skip seeing this at the checkout counter."

———

EVE

I HAD my laptop in my arms, the camera and memory card case in my bag. I had to take them to the station to meet Nix and Shane. I'd told Nix about what I had found, what I'd seen on the memory cards. I hadn't realized they were evidence in a murder investigation until I got home and viewed them. Had I known what I was going to discover, I'd have used gloves, gotten an evidence bag to put them in.

But I was glad I'd seen it first. God, I hadn't found the file of me and Shane from earlier, and I'd gone through them all more than once. I didn't feel relieved, because I was still panicked I'd missed it somehow and someone at the station would find it. As soon as I turned these things over, it would be evidence. And my fun morning sex would be available to all.

Nix had volunteered to pick up Shane and bring him to the station for questioning. I couldn't do it. Not only because it was now a conflict of interest, but because I wasn't sure if I'd shoot him on sight. Or cry. I had powerful evidence that implicated Shane in the murder of Erin Mills.

Means. He'd had sex with her on several occasions

with no one ever knowing. He'd think it easy to do so again.

Motive. She threatened on film to out him. The film put him with Erin three days before her death. She'd mentioned the time he'd taken her virginity—underage—and I had that film too. It showed a yearslong trend of behavior against women. Erin was the only one who'd been murdered though.

I clicked the fob on my key chain to unlock my car. Something wasn't right about it all. Not the obvious, Shane filming all those women. I couldn't deny what I'd found myself. What I'd seen with my own eyes on those memory cards. All the women he'd slept with, including me. That didn't even include what he'd done so ruthlessly to Erin. God, that was awful, what he'd done. I wasn't used to dealing with a man like this, so I wasn't looking at it all correctly.

I was seeing it from the eyes of a victim. I was his latest since I'd just had sex with him in that same bed in the same way as the video. God, he hadn't even touched me, just let me use him. I'd thought it hot at the time. He'd kept his hands behind his head. It had seemed as if he had to tuck them there to control himself. Now it was clear he'd done so to keep them out of the camera's way.

Out of the camera's way.

I stopped just in front of my car. Stood on the sidewalk. Thought hard. Shane hadn't been seen in the films. Not one of them, or at least in the ones I'd gone through, and that had been a lot. Only a hint of leg, groin. Like this morning, Shane had kept himself from being part of the shot because he'd wanted the camera to pick up me and only me.

Shane had wanted every one of the clips to be of the woman and the woman only because it was like a trophy to him. To see his conquest in all her naked glory. To know he could fuck her, expose her and get away with it.

But maybe that wasn't it. Or that wasn't *only* it. Maybe it was because he didn't want to be filmed. Maybe because he didn't want anyone to know it was him in the films.

Blackmail? Shane had money. Millions if I took a guess, from his dad. But he'd said he didn't touch any of it. He could have blackmailed the women and added it to his account, and it wouldn't stand out. But why would a man who had access to all that money want to extort more?

Maybe because it wasn't *Shane* in the films. I turned around and raced back inside.

I dropped my laptop on my desk, pulled out the memory cards. I grabbed one, set it in the little adapter and then put it in the slot. No, not that one. I switched it. Clicked through the files until I found the one I was looking for. The one where the woman had turned around to reverse cowgirl, to when Shane had spanked her. I slid the bar across the bottom of the file to move quickly through the video, passed the spank and went back to it.

There.

His thumb slipped into her ass, and I didn't pay attention to what was happening, only the ring on the right ring finger. Gold. A few diamonds. Nothing I'd seen Shane wear.

I closed the file, switched memory cards to the most recent one. I found the file by date, the one of Shane and Erin right before her death. I slid the bar forward until she started talking. She threatened. "I wonder if everyone will want to know you like underage girls."

A hand settled on her thigh for less than two seconds. Again, the ring.

"Oh my God," I said, trying to use the laptop's track pad with shaking hands. I went to a browser, typed in the name of the person I now knew had killed Erin.

Eddie Nickel.

Loads of pictures of the famous movie star filled

the page. I scrolled through until I found one of him standing at a movie premiere, clicked on it.

There, on his right hand, was the ring.

Shane hadn't fucked any of those women. Shane hadn't killed Erin Mills. His father had.

12

HANE

"OKAY, I'M HERE."

I dropped into the chair in one of the interrogation rooms of the police department.

Crossing my arms over my chest, I slouched.

The drive into town had been silent. What could I say? What *should* I say? He hadn't mentioned the need for a lawyer, but if they had video proof I had sex with Erin Mills, then I wasn't sure what legal counsel could do.

I may have had sex with a number of women in Cutthroat, but not Erin Mills. She was Lucas's little sister. I'd grown up with her, remembered when she was a kid. Not only was there some kind of guy code about fucking a friend's sister, but I'd never been interested.

Erin had been vain. She'd been into the whole rich Cutthroat circle that I avoided like the plague. She'd never been my type, although I hadn't realized what my type was until I met Eve Miranski. *She* was my type. If Erin were still alive, she wouldn't turn my head, no matter how pretty.

Nix took a seat across from me, dropped a notepad and pen onto the table, pressed a button on the machine set to the side.

"This is Nix Knight. Interview starting at twelve thirty-seven. Please state your name for the record."

I stared at him for a second, then took a breath. "Shane Nickel."

"Did you know Erin Mills?"

"Yes."

"Explain your relationship."

"We didn't have a *relationship*. I'm friends with Lucas Mills, her brother. She is... *was* a few years younger. Just like you, I spent time at their house, so I saw her there. Also around town. Skiing. At a summer festival or something, but we never went together."

"You never had any kind of personal relationship with her?"

"You mean did we date?"

"You describe it."

I liked Nix better when he wasn't being a fucking detective. "I did not date Erin Mills."

"A fling then."

I thought of Eve and how she'd wanted no strings.

"No fling, no dates, nothing. I don't think I was ever alone with her."

"So you didn't have sex."

I glanced up at the ceiling tiles, took a moment. "I never had sex with Erin Mills. I never touched her with her clothes on, her clothes off or anywhere in between. As I said, I don't think I was ever alone with her."

"For the record, you never had sexual intercourse with Erin Mills."

I widened my eyes and stared at Nix. Really? How many times could I answer the same question.

"No."

"When was the last time you saw Erin?"

I paused, considered. "Maybe over the summer at one of my sister's parties. Only in passing. I didn't speak with her, and that's why I can't remember exactly."

"That's about six months or so?"

"Yes. Okay, I answered your questions, now tell me what the hell is going on."

"We have video of you and Erin Mills having sex."

"Impossible."

"More than once."

"Again, impossible."

"You offered her a spot in one of your father's movies in exchange for sex."

I sat up, set my forearms on the table, looked really closely at Nix so he could understand. "There is no way I would have offered her a spot in an Eddie Nickel film."

"Why's that?"

"Because I've never done it. Not once. Never. I hate my dad. I wouldn't send anyone I knew his way. Especially a woman."

"Why's that?"

I took another deep breath. I'd never shared my family history. Finch knew, but he'd seen my dad go off in a rage when we were younger.

"Eddie Nickel might come across as a nice guy, but he's a monster. He used to beat us. Me, Poppy. For years. I'd never send a woman in his direction because if he beat his own kids, I wouldn't doubt he'd beat her too."

Nix pulled his cell from his shirt pocket, fiddled with it, then set it on the table. A video played. I looked down at it, saw a porno. I picked it up, recognized it as Erin Mills. It was a strange video, as if someone had taken a video of their laptop that had a film of Erin Mills having sex on the screen. A video of a video. "For the record, I'm showing a clip of Erin Mills having sex with Shane Nickel."

I winced, not interested in seeing Erin naked. "It's not me. I never had sex with her."

"Is that your bedroom?"

It was hard to get past the fucking to see the bed and walls behind, but I recognized the placement of the doors, my bedspread. "Yes."

Jesus, what the fuck? That was my bedroom.

"Is that Erin Mills?" Nix asked.

Obviously. "Yes."

"Explain."

"Where did you get this?"

"Detective Eve Miranski found it."

"Where?"

"In your bedroom."

"Are you kidding me?"

Nix didn't mention why Eve had been in my bedroom to find it. I wasn't going to put that on the record. I had to guess he was intentionally keeping her personal life out of public case records, and I was thankful for that.

"Cut the recording, Nix." He didn't do anything. "Please."

He pushed the button on the table.

"Thanks. You know I'm in a relationship with Eve."

"Yeah, and that's why this freaks me the fuck out. There's a different video of you having sex with Erin when she was sixteen. Took her virginity."

"Holy fuck." I shook my head. "It wasn't me. Jesus, it wasn't me."

"Then let's figure this out." He grabbed his cell, turned off the clip of Erin. "I shouldn't be doing this, but even with all the evidence Eve found, I believe you."

"Eve found what, a memory card or something this morning?"

"She found a hidden camera behind the picture over your bed."

My mouth dropped open. "Are you shitting me?"

He shook his head.

"With it were memory cards of conquests. Hundreds of them. Including Erin Mills seven years ago and also three days before her death." He tipped his chin toward his cell. "If you watch the rest of that video, Erin reminds you of the recording you did of her when she was younger, that she didn't get a movie deal. She threatens you, stating you give her a film role now or she'll out you for underage sex."

My head was spinning. I stood, paced.

"There was a hidden camera in my bedroom."

"Yes."

"There are hundreds of videos of sex happening there. Holy fuck. Do you see me in the films?"

He shook his head. "No. The camera is positioned so that only the women are visible. Your legs are shown a little. Thighs. Dark leg hair. A little bit of groin."

I flinched at the picture he made. "I never stay there. Finch can account for that. Last time was over the summer. I pretty much live out at the cabin where you picked me up. The house in town sits empty. Any of my friends know that."

Nix nodded. "I remember you mentioning that in the past."

I sighed, glad I wasn't losing my shit. "This has been happening for years?"

"How could you miss sex happening in your own bed? I mean, if I went on vacation and people used my bed while I was gone, I'd know when I got back."

"Would you? If someone cleaned up after

themselves... like a hotel. I don't want to think about how many people fuck in the beds we stay in."

Nix pursed his lips at the thought. "Then who?"

I froze. My thoughts quieted. Focused. My stomach dropped. "Holy fuck."

"What?"

I looked at Nix. "There's one person who has women dropping at his feet. One person who has a movie deal bargaining chip in his power. One person who knows I don't stay in the house. One person who would love knowing he pulled one over on me... for years, by fucking his conquests in my own bed."

I could tell the moment he caught on. "Seriously?"

"My father is an asshole. He's a narcissist. I wouldn't put this past him. God, it all fits. I'm sure I can give alibis for at least some of the dates on those videos. No one's checked for prints in my house because, well, who would think to test? I bet my dad's prints are all over that room."

I ran my hand over my hair. Fucking pissed. My father had fucked women, and underaged girls, in my bed.

"Holy shit, he killed Erin."

Nix stood, his chair scraping across the floor. "I think you're right."

After he grabbed his cell, he opened the door and

went out into the hall. I followed. He looked across the room. "Where's Eve?" he asked someone at a nearby desk.

The man shrugged. "Haven't seen her."

I looked to Nix.

"She was going to come in while I went to get you. Interview you. She can't do it since there's a conflict of interest." He cleared his throat and offered a raised eyebrow.

"There sure as fuck is a conflict of interest. Now where's my woman?"

I checked my cell. Nothing. Nix did the same. "There's a voice mail."

He put the phone to his ear. Listened. I knew the second something was wrong by the look on his face. He glanced down at the screen.

"She called twenty minutes ago."

"Let me listen to that."

He pushed a button, then held the phone out for me to take.

I missed the very beginning in the handoff. "—and I went back and looked at the videos. I was wrong. It's not Shane. God, it's so scary. There's a hand that comes into the film with Erin right before her murder. There's a ring. A ring that Eddie Nickel wears. It's all over social media photos. I went back to the old film of

Erin, and he touches her then, too. The ring's there. I found it in one more clip, too. Another woman I don't know. It's him. It's Eddie Nickel. I'm going to the ranch to question him. I need you to come. Bring backup because I want this legit. I don't want him getting off on a technicality because I'm in love with his son."

I looked up at Nix.

"Holy shit." She was in love with me, and she told *Nix* on a voice mail.

"Yeah, holy shit," he replied. "That was twenty minutes ago, and she's confronting a murderer."

Eve was going to see my father. The one man in the world I hated. Until today, for what he did to me and Poppy. And now? Now he had so many more sins. The woman I loved was going to be alone with a murderer, and I never had a chance to tell her how I felt.

"Finch is at his ranch. He's closer than we are."

"He's not police," Nix said as he ran down the hall toward the front entrance.

"Like I give a shit," I told him, keeping pace. "We'll call him on the way to get his ass over there."

13

VE

VOICE MAIL. I'd gotten Nix's voice mail. I should have called it in, but I knew he'd get here quick. I couldn't believe I'd thought Shane had been with all those women, done those awful things with them. Used them. And Erin... God, how could I have thought him capable of murdering her?

It had all been right there on the films. But it hadn't been him.

I pulled up in front of Eddie Nickel's huge mansion. It was the biggest log cabin I'd ever seen. Two stories with wings and a separate garage with five stalls. The landscaping was buried under two feet of snow, but I was sure it was gorgeous in the summer. There was a circular driveway in front, and the pavement was heated. A rarity in Montana since it was costly, but it kept the driveway warm so it didn't need shoveling. Something a guy like Eddie Nickel would have.

I climbed from the car, went up the front steps and rang the doorbell.

My breath was caught in my throat, and I let it out. Took another deep breath, yoga breathing, to calm my racing heart. I remembered what I saw, knew the guy I was confronting had done all that.

The door opened. No butler, but Eddie Nickel himself. I'd seen him in movies, occasionally around town, but at a distance. He looked just like in the films, although admittedly a little better. Midfifties. Black hair with a little gray threaded in at the temples. If he colored it, I couldn't tell. If he had Botox to diminish wrinkles around his eyes and across his forehead, I couldn't tell that either. He looked naturally good in a pale blue dress shirt and jeans.

The ring I'd seen in the films was on his finger. Adrenaline kicked in at the sight of it. That gaudy thing was his downfall. The difference between freedom and a jail cell.

A stupid gold ring.

He smiled at me, then looked me over, completely unaware he'd been caught.

Yeah, he'd used all those women. I felt skeeved out by that quick perusal. He'd never met me, didn't know who I was, but was assessing me to fuck.

I took a deep breath, faked a smile and said, "Hi, Mr. Nickel, I'm Eve Miranski."

"Come in."

He stepped back and allowed me entrance, having no idea why I was here. He didn't care.

He headed toward the back of the house, and I followed, passing a sweeping staircase and a den. Pictures of himself were all over the walls. Photos, paintings and posters of his movies covered every surface. I didn't see one family photo.

The great room was sunken. He took two steps down to the large seating area that faced a massive stone fireplace and enormous windows with views of Montana. I could probably see to Utah from here.

"We haven't met. I'd have remembered you," he said, turning to face me. "Sit, please."

He held out his hand, indicating a white sofa. I settled onto it, and he took a spot across from me, a glass coffee table the size of a car between us.

"No, we haven't met," I replied. "I wanted to ask

you a few questions about your relationships, specifically with Erin Mills."

His smile slipped a little, but he was a good actor. "Are you with the press? You know I love to give interviews, but usually they're arranged with my publicist." He shrugged and studied me. "You're here, though, so I'll forgive you."

If you let me fuck you over this couch, he was probably thinking.

"I'm with the Cutthroat Police."

He cocked his head to the side as if he were a dog and heard me say, *Walk.*

"You asked after Erin Mills. She was the event planner for the film that was shot here in Cutthroat over the summer and fall."

"You knew her well then?"

He shrugged. "There are so many people on set. I knew her, of course."

"Did you ever meet her casually, perhaps for a date?"

He grinned. "Did you see it in the papers? The tabloids?"

I offered him a small smile. "No."

"Then I didn't."

"Surely not everything you do is shared with the press."

"You got in my house, didn't you?"

"You let me in," I countered.

"I try to be a private person, but someone with my... exposure makes it difficult."

"You didn't meet Erin then, in secret?"

"No."

"Not even to offer her a role in one of your films?"

"There are enough talent scouts out there to do that job. Besides, she worked for the film as the event planner."

"She didn't want to be *in* the film instead of behind the scenes? She was pretty. I'd think the camera would have really liked her."

His eyes narrowed ever so slightly at that.

"Why all these questions about that poor girl?"

"I'm investigating her murder. It's my job to find the killer."

"How's that going?"

I sat quietly for a moment. "Getting really close."

———

FINCH

.   .   .

"ARE you fucking telling me that Eve is at the house of a murderer. Alone?"

I ran from the stable to the house, trying not to bust my ass on the path, which was covered in compacted snow. I'd used the snowblower to clear it, but it wouldn't see bare ground for months.

"Yes. We're twenty minutes out if Nix would put his foot to the floor. You're less than ten. Move it." Shane's voice was tense and sharp, as if it could cut glass.

I shot through the mudroom and grabbed the keys to my truck off the counter, then headed right back out.

"Explain to me what the fuck is going on."

I climbed into the truck, got it started and gunned the engine. Having a dually had its advantages, and I was glad for the extra wheels, the weight and power. The cell connection to the truck's dashboard kicked in, and Shane's voice came through the speakers. I dropped my cell into the center console and had a death grip on the steering wheel as I punched it down the driveway.

"Eve found a hidden camera in my bedroom. It had memory cards with it. She checked them out and found hundreds of videos of him having sex with women."

"Why didn't she just send in the cavalry? Why is she there alone?"

"Because the video is just of the women. The guy's hidden."

What the fuck was he talking about? "Explain."

He did. I drove as he shared how Eddie had positioned the camera so he was never seen. He had the women on top for all the sex. Nix cut in and added that it appeared the women didn't know they were filmed.

"It's like a trophy," I guessed. "Fucking a woman and keeping the record of it. He'd love the fact that they had no clue it had been done. And the kicker is, he did it in *your* bed."

"Exactly," Shane replied. He went on to explain the clip of Erin threatening Eddie.

"Jesus. He's a sick fuck. He manipulated a sixteen-year-old girl, and when she finally had enough and got pissed about it, he kills her. Why is Eve all alone?"

"She didn't want to review the memory cards at the station," Nix said. "She took them to her house and went through them there."

"Last night." Shane's two words prompted me to remember what we'd done together, in the same bed where all the films had been recorded. If Nix hadn't known we were a thing before, he was well aware now. "And this morning. Just like the others."

Just like the others. They'd fucked and she'd been on top. Yeah, Nix had a pretty good idea why Eve had kept the videos out of the station.

"She thought she was one in a long line," I said, realizing what Eve must have imagined. "Holy fuck. You said hundreds. She thought you had sex with all those women, filming them without their knowledge?"

"Yes."

"And what happened to Erin... all after what her ex did to her."

"What did her ex do?" Nix asked, his voice dark.

"Get in line," Shane replied.

Yeah, if we came across this Chad fucker, Nix could have what was left of him after Shane and I were through. On top of how sick the whole thing was, I could only imagine the betrayal she'd felt at thinking it had been Shane.

"How'd she figure out it wasn't you?"

He told me about her seeing Eddie's ring, that ugly fucking thing he never took off. How she put it all together. Erin at sixteen, Erin as the event planner for his local film. The threat she'd made.

"If Eve brought the camera and memory cards to the station, it would be evidence. Hell, it still is regardless," Nix said. "I'm guessing there might be something in there she doesn't want shared?"

It was silent for a moment, and I had to assume Shane nodded or gave some nonverbal yes.

"If it's on there, we'll get it taken out. You have my word."

"I don't give a shit about the recording. I'm proud of how my woman looks when I'm fucking her. But I don't want it to be the only thing I have left of her. Can't this fucking SUV go any faster?" Shane shouted at Nix.

"I'm five minutes out," I said but wondered if it was soon enough.

If Eddie Nickel was fucked up enough to secretly film fucking dozens of women in his own son's bed and murder one of them in cold blood, then he wouldn't hesitate to finish the one person who could destroy it all.

———

EVE

EDDIE STOOD UP. "WANT SOME COFFEE?"

He didn't wait for an answer and headed for the

kitchen. I stood as well but followed at a slower pace. I watched him in his... natural habitat. His huge mansion, his oversize kitchen with sleek appliances, his fancy coffee maker that hissed and had more buttons than the space shuttle. He didn't look like a murderer. He didn't look like a rapist. Handsome didn't describe him. He was charismatic. Confident. Brash, even.

He knew he had power, especially over women, and that came out just shy of cocky. It appeared every single one of those women on the secret video, aside from any that were underage, had consented to sex. They'd wanted to sleep with the famous movie star, Eddie Nickel.

He'd given them what they wanted, but had done so because *he'd* gotten what he wanted. Video trophies of his conquest. A shrine of sorts to his ability to outwit as many women as he could.

He'd gotten away with it for years. Probably longer than the collection of memory cards. Technology changed. There had to be VCR tapes somewhere of even earlier conquests.

His life was a role. Right now he was on a stage of sorts, showing me the Eddie Nickel he wanted me to see. As soon as the police got here, he was going to up his acting chops, probably give an Oscar-worthy performance. I wanted to get a glimpse of the real man. The man Shane and Poppy knew.

"I have to give you a lot of credit," I said. The kitchen opened into the great room with a wide counter, probably fifteen feet long, as a divider. I leaned against the granite on the great room side. Eddie Nickel was on the other side, at the far end working the machine.

He looked my way with a patented smile. I was surprised a sparkle didn't reflect off the veneers. "Oh?"

"You almost got away with it."

"With what?"

"Killing Erin Mills."

His smile dropped, and he frowned but focused on the hot brew dripping into a mug.

"She was the only woman who figured it out. Isn't that right?" I asked. "All the others had no clue. Still don't."

He turned, leaned against the counter, coffee forgotten. "I don't know what you're talking about."

"I'd have thought, with all your experience with the ladies, that you wouldn't mess with a woman scorned. You should have given her a role in one of your films."

There was a shift in him, so slight I wouldn't have noticed if I hadn't been focused on him.

"Everyone earns a spot in my movies because of their skill."

"Women earn theirs on their backs, right?" I countered, then held up one finger. "No, wait. On top. That's how you like it. The woman's always on top."

"Not in my world," he said. Yeah, there was the real Eddie Nickel. His voice was deeper, his tone cold.

"No, not in your world. But in your secret films they are. Every. Single. One."

I wanted to get this asshole to talk. I wanted to know why. Maybe then I could understand Chad and how he'd almost destroyed me.

I'd almost let him, too, if it weren't for Shane and Finch. If they hadn't shown me Chad still had a hold on my life, blocking myself off from love. Shane somehow had allowed me in even with what his dad had done to him. He'd sought out love, *real* love, instead of avoiding it. Finch had fought against a guy just like Chad and Eddie Nickel. A misogynist who believed he held all the power. It had been validated when Finch had gone off to jail even while being honorable.

Shane deserved the full truth about his father. Finch needed to see an asshole get the justice.

I stared him down. He knew it was over, that all his secrets were known. It was time to poke the bear.

"I'm surprised you were afraid of Erin."

He gave a dry laugh and slowly shook his head. "Afraid?"

"She was the only woman who'd stood up to you. To get what she wanted from you. What she deserved."

"Deserved? She didn't deserve a role in my film. She wasn't good enough."

"She earned that role when she was sixteen and you raped her."

"Rape? She was there all on her own. She wanted it."

He made me sick.

"It took her a few years, but she had power over you."

His eyes flared. Not with heat but cold. Bitter cold. "She held *no* power."

"You lost your cool. Went to her house. Hit her with the glass award."

I held my breath. This was it. He'd admitted to being with a sixteen-year-old Erin, but would he admit to killing her?

"She's dead. Who has the power now?"

Taking his time, he walked out of the kitchen and into the great room. I turned to face him but kept my back to the counter.

"Eddie Nickel, you are under arrest for the murder of Erin Mills."

He laughed, this time a full, real one. "You're arresting me? A woman."

I knew the signs. Knew how he talked. Baiting me to get angry, to prove his point and then turn it around on me as being my fault. A narcissist and a sociopath.

"We can wait for the male members of the Cutthroat police to show up. That won't change the charges. Or this." I pulled my small recorder I used for when I interviewed people and needed to listen again or share it with others, like Nix. In this case I wanted insurance that while a confession might be collected outside of the regular channels, I had something.

"Ironic, isn't it? You being recorded without knowing? How's it feel?"

He cocked his head to the side, studied me. Then the real Eddie Nickel came out, approaching me with a speed that was surprising. "If it's being recorded, then one more for old times' sake. Fucking the detective on the case might just get me off." The grin he gave me was pure evil. "In more ways than one."

Before I could do more than move to the right, he grabbed the back of my neck and yanked, pulling me into him. His body was hard, sturdy, his grip strong. Hot breath fanned my face as he glared down at me.

Fingers dug into my skin, and his grip was ruthless. "My lawyers will have you painted the slut, asking for it. Begging to be with *Eddie Nickel*. Conflict of interest wanting my dick, taking the evidence for a ride. The case will be dismissed."

I intentionally raised my knee slowly so he'd sense what I was going to do. He turned his hips to shield his groin, and I only kneed him in the thigh. He grinned, thinking he'd bested me. Then I dropped my weight and brought my heel down on top of his foot.

Like most Montanans in the winter, he'd left his shoes in a mudroom, closet or near an outside door so as not to track snow and mud around the house. Eddie Nickel was only wearing socks. And since I was a guest, I'd kept my boots on. Also like most Montanans, I wore sturdy leather boots with solid heels. The boots could be worn anywhere—in a stable, on the back of a horse or even in the house of a murderer.

His hold on my neck dropped, and he howled in pain as he bent at the waist. Stepping to the left, I pivoted, hooking his wrist and wrapping it around behind him. The move was just like what I'd done to Finch, but this time I wasn't gentle. I wrenched his arm so his shoulder was just shy of coming out of the socket and forced him to the floor.

I leaned in toward his ear, my hand on his wrist,

my knee jammed into his spine and all my weight on him. His face was turned to the side, and he didn't look confident any longer. "Remember this moment, asshole. And by the way," I said, pressing even harder into his back. "I do like it on top."

The front door burst open. In came Finch—out of breath and eyes wild—and he watched as I grabbed my handcuffs from the holder on my belt and slapped them on Eddie Nickel.

Finch set his hands on his hips and took a deep breath. I watched as his shoulders dropped. He grinned. "Sugar, glad as fuck you're wearing clothes this time."

14

 HANE

My father was in jail for murdering Erin Mills. With the camera and memory card evidence, other charges would pile up. Sex with a minor. Voyeurism. I had a feeling that wasn't all. It sickened me to think of all that he'd done, that he'd been evil to more than just me and Poppy.

"You okay?" I asked my sister.

We were at the diner, and she sat across from me. It was after the dinner rush, so there weren't many in the place. The scent of fries filled the air, but I wasn't hungry. She'd been stirring her coffee for the past five minutes, but I wasn't going to comment. Looking up, she gave me a small smile. "Yeah."

"Yeah," I repeated. I was totally okay with him being in jail. He belonged there for what he'd done to us alone. But it would take me a while to get my head around the extent of his... evil. He truly was evil. The number of women he'd hurt, knowingly and unknowingly. They'd all be identified, then notified of what had been done to them.

Eve sat next to me, Finch on her other side. Right where she belonged.

Nix and I got to my father's house about two minutes after Finch. Nix had broken most land speed records to get there. Eve had been fine—she'd taken care of my father all by herself—while Finch had looked like he'd aged five years. I knew exactly how he felt.

My father had been transported to the station in one of the backup cars and processed. I hadn't said a word to him, could barely look his way as he'd been dragged off. Nix had collected the camera and memory cards from Erin's car and brought them into my father's house. While we'd figured there wouldn't be any videos of us with Eve on the camera since it hadn't been turned on, we'd confirmed that before he stuck it all in an evidence bag and took it to the station.

I'd driven Eve in her car back to town. I wasn't letting her out of my sight. Nix and Finch followed in their own vehicles. The station was in chaos when we arrived. Everyone was put on the Mills case. One crew was sent to Eddie Nickel's house to look for evidence. Another crew was sent to mine to tackle my bedroom where all the filming had occurred. Finch and I had been questioned by the chief himself, since it was all hands on deck, taking our statements and having us sign off on them. Only then were we free to go, although we didn't go anywhere. No fucking way were we leaving Eve.

I'd wanted to spank her ass for going to my father's place alone, but I was too fucking relieved to find her unharmed. Once Eve was done with her work for the day, we'd called Poppy to meet her at the diner. This wasn't information to give over the phone, and I didn't want her to be alone when she learned the truth.

After we laid it all out for her, she didn't even cry. Barely blinked, although I knew she was stunned. It was going to take a while to process. The mayor had a news conference scheduled for eight, and that meant the media would go nuts. They'd descend on Cutthroat like buzzards on a carcass.

"I'm going to go away. Leave Cutthroat for a while," Poppy finally said. We looked to her, waited for her to say more. "I can't handle the media."

She'd been thinking the same as me.

I nodded. "Good idea."

"I'll go see Fiona, my friend from college. Can't get much farther away from home than Perth, Australia."

"It's summer down there," I said.

She smiled for the first time since I'd shared the news. "I could use a good tan."

Nix came in, pulled out a chair and sat beside me. "Holy shit," he murmured, wiping a hand down his face.

Beneath the table, Eve took my hand in hers, gave it a squeeze.

Nix pointed at Eve. "You pull shit like that again, I'll take you over my knee. I don't give a shit if your men kill me."

"Get in line," Finch said, eyes snapping with frustration, the same way I felt at what could have happened to Eve.

"Hey!" she said, taking offense.

Nix nodded, paying her no attention. "Good."

Kit came over, wrapped an arm around Nix and kissed his temple. She was in the diner's T-shirt and jeans and had been working tables on the other side of the restaurant. From what I'd heard, she was keeping her job at the diner while her party planner business took off. She'd had to start over on her own since Erin had been killed. "I'm done for the day."

Donovan arrived next, and he slid a table over to make ours bigger to fit everyone, then took a seat. He tugged Kit down onto his lap. "Kitty Kat," he said, then gave her a quick kiss.

I glanced at Eve, who had a look of... envy on her face? Was she jealous of what Kit shared with her men? She shouldn't be. She had the same thing with us. Maybe it took a sociopathic murderer to make her realize it.

Finch looked my way, gave me a small nod.

"My father's with the Mills family," Donovan said. "He wanted to tell them personally the murderer had been caught."

Of course he did. Everyone at the table knew Donovan's dad wanted all the glory.

"What about Lucas?" Nix asked.

"He was with them but left. He's got Cy and Hailey. He's not alone," Donovan confirmed.

Finch looked my way, gave me a small nod. We were done here. Poppy wasn't alone. Nix and Donovan would watch out for her. But Finch and I needed to be with Eve. Only Eve.

"We'll be at Finch's for a while," I said, pushing my chair back to stand. "As soon as the police release my house, I'm selling it. Burning it to the ground. I don't give a shit."

"We'll deal with the media," Nix said. "I'll have someone on Poppy."

She shook her head. "I'll hire security until I leave town. Eddie Nickel can pay for it."

Her eyes were fierce. She was angry, not sad, and that was where she needed to be. She looked my way. "Go. Take care of Eve."

"I'm fine," Eve replied. She hadn't said much since we'd left the station. "My mind's just working through everything."

Finch took her hand and tugged her up against him, wrapping her in a tight hold. "I know just the way to shut that pretty head of yours off."

I couldn't agree more. "Let's go," I said, heading out of the diner and leaving everyone behind.

———

EVE

. . .

THE MUDROOM DOOR clicked closed behind us. Shane had driven my car—he'd given me a male death stare when I pulled out my keys—to Finch's house, and Finch had followed in his big truck. There was so much to do on the Mills case, but for now my work was done. I'd filled out the paperwork, the reports turned in. The memory cards would be searched by the tech team and analyzed. The women would be identified and notified. They would be witnesses in Eddie Nickel's trial, if it ever happened.

It was possible his lawyers would make a deal. He wouldn't get less than life for what he'd done. Not only because of premeditated murder but the pile of other felonies the DA would be sure to include. Was justice served? I had no idea. But Erin Mills's life had been destroyed long before Eddie Nickel had hit her with her volunteer award. He'd ruined it when she was sixteen.

Finch hung his hat on the hook by the door, then looked to me.

"It's time to talk, sugar."

I took a deep breath, let it out.

"Yeah, I know."

I felt like a teenager caught out after curfew. Worse.

"You scared the shit out of me. Do you have any

idea how I felt when Shane called me and told me you were at the house of a murderer?"

I looked down at the wood floor, my socked feet.

Shane spoke up. "Even if he wasn't the guy who'd killed Erin and secretly recorded fucking half of Cutthroat, you knew about my dad. I told you he was violent. That he hit women. Kids."

"He had to be put away. I know this sounds lame, but I tried calling Nix."

Shane paced. "There's no reception for a stretch between my cabin and town. Like Nix said, we should spank your ass, make sure you don't sit for a week and remember you're not John Wayne."

I looked to Shane, tipped my chin up. "For a guy who got smacked around as a kid, you want to lay a hand on me?"

Shane looked grim. "Don't compare what my dad did with what Finch and I are going to do to you."

Glancing between them, they had similar expressions. Anger, hurt, frustration, desire. My lips were suddenly dry. "What... what are you going to do?"

"Show you how much you mean to us," Finch said. "Hell, we've only known you a few days, but we told you, first thing. When you know, you know. Today proved that life is short, that there's no reason to waste time when what you want is right in front of you."

"What do you want?" I asked. My heart was in my throat, and for once I was eager for the dominance in his tone.

"You," Shane said, taking a step toward me. "On Nix's voice mail you said you loved me. Is that true?"

I looked to him, nodded. My heart was wide open, ready to be held or crushed. "I... I think so. I've never felt this way before. About both of you." I looked to Finch, made sure he knew he was included in my words.

"Good. We're not letting you go," Shane said.

"Being tossed in jail didn't change my mind about watching out for those I care about," Finch stated. "If handcuffing you to my bed will keep you safe, I'll do it."

"Living with a guy who beat the shit out of me didn't make me grow up to be like him," Shane added. "The opposite. I protect what's mine. You. I agree with Finch. And don't for a second think us being possessive means we're anything like your ex."

I sighed, smiled. I didn't feel the walls I'd put around my heart. I didn't fight the feelings I had for these two. For once I let go. Gave in. Opened my heart.

They could be as possessive as they wanted because they were wrapping me in love, not control.

"I know. I want... I want you both. Completely. Not just for sex. For a relationship. For... well, maybe forever."

The tension left their bodies like air from a balloon.

Finch came over, tucked my hair back. "We'll take forever, sugar, but let's start with today."

"Now," Shane added, pressing into my side. "The real world will creep back in soon enough. For now let's forget."

I nodded and kissed Shane. I didn't hold back, showed him through the kiss that I was all in. I pulled back, turned to Finch and kissed him as well. Both of them needed to know how I felt. Words weren't enough.

"Want to fuck here on the kitchen counter or in bed?" Shane asked.

"Bed," I said, pulling back from Finch's lips.

Finch led me to his bedroom, and between the two of them, they stripped me. Then I took turns helping them out of their clothes. Only when we were bare, body and soul, did we tumble into bed.

Hands roamed over me. I didn't know who was touching me where, only that my nipples were being sucked and plucked, my pussy caressed, fingers sliding in to ready me for their big cocks.

"Soon, sugar, we'll take you together. I'll take your ass, Shane your pussy."

I writhed between them, so ready. "No, now."

They stilled. "We're big and we haven't gotten you prepared."

"I want to try," I admitted. I'd loved it when their fingers had been inside me there. The idea of a cock...

Finch shifted and tugged open the bedside drawer to grab a bottle of lube. "We'll play first, see how that goes."

"Hands and knees," Shane said. They shifted out of the way to give me room to turn. Once I was in position, Shane dropped onto the bed, the mattress dipping with his weight. "Come here."

I moved to the right, lifted a knee and climbed over him so while I was still on my hands and knees, I straddled him. The air was cool on my heated skin. I knew they could see every inch of me, but I wasn't embarrassed. The way they looked at me made me feel pretty, made me feel desired. Wanted.

And that made me bold.

Shane's cock was right there, and instead of kissing him, I gave him a wicked grin and held his gaze as I shifted lower. His hips bucked as I licked him, then took him into my mouth.

"Shit, woman."

Yeah, I felt *very* bold. But then a cold drizzle of lube dripped down over my back entrance. "Easy, sugar," Finch said as he began to play. A finger slipped into my pussy and worked me like a cock would... hopefully soon. Another finger pressed against my slick entrance, carefully warming me up, pressing gently in and pulling back. Over and over until I relaxed as I sucked Shane's cock.

I lifted my head and moaned when Finch got a finger to open me up and slip in. My eyes fell closed, and I breathed through it.

"Ready for another finger?" Finch asked as he dribbled more lube and worked it in.

I nodded, then looked to Shane. He cupped my cheek, and I licked his dick, then went back to work. I could suck him and allow Finch to play.

It was Shane, though, who lifted me off him a little while later. He tugged me up to kiss me; then he looked in my eyes. "I want in that pussy when I come."

Finch kept his fingers in me but rested his palm against my lower back. He kept it there as I sank down onto Shane.

"Oh my God," I moaned, Shane so big in my pussy and Finch with two fingers in my ass.

Somehow they found a rhythm that had them alternating inside me. I'd thought it was good with one guy, but this?

"More," I breathed.

Shane watched me closely, his jaw clenched tight, the cords in his neck taut. Sweat beaded his brow. He was holding back.

I looked over my shoulder. Finch was right there, and I kissed him. "Please. I want you, too."

"Sugar," he groaned. He didn't say anything for a minute, only watched me. "I'll go slow. You tell me if it's too much."

I nodded and he slipped his fingers from me. Instantly I felt empty, even with Shane inside me. It wasn't enough. One of them wasn't enough anymore. I needed them both. Together. Now.

"Give Shane a kiss," Finch said, and I turned, lowered myself down so my body was pressed to Shane's. Shane cupped my cheek and kissed me, his legs slowly widening, which opened me up even more. For Finch.

I felt Finch shift behind me, his hand on my bottom, pulling my cheeks apart. A second later it wasn't his fingers at my back entrance, but his dick, hard and big and slick with lube, insistent.

"Breathe," Shane whispered. I did as he said. "Good girl. Again."

He kept talking to me, soothing me as Finch added more lube, pressed, then popped in.

I gasped, my eyes widening at... "Holy shit," I whispered, trying to breathe past the feeling of having both of them inside me. Finch was so much bigger than his two fingers, and it burned a little, the stretch.

"I'm so full."

"Sugar," Finch growled, his hand gripping my hip. "You're so fucking hot. Tight. I'm not going to last."

"Me either," Shane said.

"I... I... oh my God," I breathed as they began to move.

It was awkward and unusual. It didn't hurt, but it was... weird because it felt so good. I had no idea I had so many places that turned me on. Combined, I was doomed.

I was going to come. My clit was pressed against Shane's hard body, and every time they rocked in and out of me, it pushed me closer to coming.

Our breathing mingled. Our sweaty skin clung. Our bodies were fused together.

We were one. Everything was forgotten except the here and now. Shane and Finch. Me, between them.

I screamed when I came, the feelings that intense. Tears streamed down my cheeks. Finch came first, swelling within me and coming with one hot burst of cum after another. Shane followed a few thrusts of his hips later, his head arched back on the pillow in his own ecstasy.

Finch carefully pulled out and moved off the bed. Shane rolled so he was on top, then pulled out. I felt the hot drips of their cum slip from me. I was sore. Achy. Blissfully relaxed.

"That was better than a spanking," I murmured into the pillow that smelled like Finch.

"Sugar, you're still going to get spanked," Finch said, naked and gorgeous. His cock was still hard, slick and shiny with his cum and lube. "But you'll get a happy ending. We promise." He turned and went into the bathroom, and I heard the shower turn on.

"Come on, let's get you cleaned up so we can get you all dirty again." Shane offered me a quick smile, one that said he was a well-fucked, well-satisfied male. He climbed from the bed and headed into bathroom as well. I'd never get tired of seeing his gorgeous bare ass.

They were mine. It had taken me years to find true

happiness. I'd thought I would be alone forever, but I knew now, that would never happen. I had two men who wanted me. For me. In all ways. They wouldn't control me. They'd have my back. No matter what life tossed at us, we'd handle it. Together. They'd walk beside me. Just as I would them.

———

Thanks for reading the Wild Mountain Men series! Hungry for more? How about some Grade-A Beefcake? Start the series with a double helping of cowboys with <u>Sir Loin Of Beef</u>.

They might call me Sir Loin of Beef, but when I see Kaitlyn for the first time, stick a fork in me, I'm done. But I won't claim her alone. Jed Cassidy and I share everything, and that includes her. If the sweet little librarian isn't ready to be wrangled by two rodeo champs, we'll just have to break her in nice and slow. She's ours. We will win her over—body and soul— and when we do? Well, let's just say we'll give her a hard ride...and it'll last a hell of a lot longer than eight seconds.

Kaitlyn Leary takes one look at the sexy cowboys and

can't remember the last time she was so eager for a double helping of... big beef. But giving in to desire might ruin everything. Because the truth is that this small town librarian isn't all she seems. Landon Duke and Jed might be talking about a future of picket fences and making babies, but the past could destroy it all. Still...two cowboys?

Who could resist?

Read <u>Sir Loin Of Beef</u> now!

NOTE FROM VANESSA

Guess what? I've got some bonus content for you with Eve, Shane and Finch. So sign up for my mailing list. There will be special bonus content for books, just for my subscribers. Signing up will let you hear about my next release as soon as it is out, too (and you get a free book...wow!)

As always...thanks for loving my books and the wild ride!

JOIN THE WAGON TRAIN!

If you're on Facebook, please join my closed group, the Wagon Train! Don't miss out on the giveaways and hot cowboys!

https://www.facebook.com/groups/
vanessavalewagontrain/

GET A FREE BOOK!

Join my mailing list to be the first to know of new releases, free books, special prices and other author giveaways.

http://freeromanceread.com

ALSO BY VANESSA VALE

For the most up-to-date listing of my books:

vanessavalebooks.com

All Vanessa Vale titles are available at Apple, Google, Kobo, Barnes & Noble, Amazon and other retailers worldwide.

ABOUT VANESSA VALE

A USA Today bestseller, Vanessa Vale writes tempting romance with unapologetic bad boys who don't just fall in love, they fall hard. Her 75+ books have sold over one million copies. She lives in the American West where she's always finding inspiration for her next story. While she's not as skilled at social media as her kids, she loves to interact with readers.

Lightning Source UK Ltd.
Milton Keynes UK
UKHW022148090223
416682UK00016B/2217